ORAL FIXATION

by Jordan Bailey

ISBN-13: 9781005137953
ISBN-10: 1477123456

Cover design by: Jordan Bailey
Library of Congress Control Number: 2018675309
Printed in the United States of America

CONTENTS

AN ORC'S PRIZE

Hence evil broods were born, Ogres, Goblins, Orcs and Giants also, who all fought with God, for which he gave them their reward.

- Beowulf

"These are dangerous times, little girl," the man gruffed with a hoarse, mocking chuckle.

Indeed, these were. Especially for Milo, who with his long auburn hair, flowing white dress and fitted black corset, had once again been mistaken for a girl. It was an ambush, a trap. And at first glance, it seemed as if a lone 'girl' had strayed too far away from home, gotten lost, and was now surrounded by a trio of grown men, each drunk and desperate and hungry. All three wore ragged clothes and tattered armor. They were bandits of some kind; dirty, smelly, and all armed with shoddy swords or knives.

"This ain't no place for a city girl like you," the second one added, his thick accent like the seafarers from the West. "Shoulda stayed at home, Lass."

Yet still what neither of them knew was that despite 'her' pretty, feminine exterior, the slight and petite 'girl' that knelt trembling in the grass was no girl at all. Indeed, what all three of them had become so worked up over was a young boy, albeit one that possessed more feminine features than male. Truth be told, hardly anyone would have seen little Milo for what he really was, especially considering his attire.

"I-I'm…" the boy meeked, his eyes darting to each of their lust-craved faces.

As the men approached, the boy took note of their weapons, then their growing bulges in each of their pants. Each of their trousers looked as if they'd burst at the seams. And as they grew closer, he could make out the distinct outline of hairy, oily genitals crammed within.

Milo used to like sneaking away from home at dusk. Through the busy streets out a secret pathway through the city walls. Outside he felt free, and he enjoyed watching the stars come out as night would fall. Then, when he knew his parents were asleep, he would sneak back home and crawl into bed, dreaming of one day embarking on his own adventures out into the world. But tonight, mere minutes after entering the woods, he suddenly found himself surrounded. It was one of the many things his mother warned him about, and the reason he was forbidden to go outside the enormous city walls. And now he knew why.

"Help!" Milo cried out in a weak, shrill voice, one that the men could never have guessed belonged to a boy. "Please! Someone!"

"Noisy little one, aintcha?" the third man, the fattest of the three mocked. He chuckled as he sheathed his knife and grabbed his crotch. "Might haveta stuff that cute 'lil mouth o' 'urs…"

"No, please, I-" Milo began, but something cut the boy off. There was movement in the trees! Was it another bandit? One that he hadn't seen before?

An all new fear took hold of Milo. Fear of the unknown. And in the dark, wooded clearing where the moonlight illuminated the silhouettes of his assailants, something else appeared. It was massive but fast, like some sort of hulking animal. It moved with silent, blinding speed behind the first bandit, but then rose from all fours, casting a black shadow over him. Soon it towered overhead, rising higher and taller on a pair of thick, tree-trunk sized legs.

Milo gasped, awestruck at the new monstrosity. *It was no animal*, he thought, as nothing he recalled could stand with such poise and stature. No, it was humanoid or humanesque, because while blanketed in shadow, he could clearly see its arms unfurling in front of him. They rippled with muscle, just as thick and terrifying as the Things legs, and in each hand was a giant, sinister axe that any normal man would have to wield with two hands.

There was a glint in the air above the hulking silhouette, metal hit by the moonlight. A second later, just as the first bandit turned, that same glinting object swung into his neck!

What followed was the swift, sickening CRUNCH of flesh and bone being cleaved in two.

The axe fell with the body, slamming into the grass with a wet THUD! Milo scurried backwards, noticing the jagged, black blade of the axe that was like no blacksmithy he had ever seen!

The second bandit lunged forward, swinging his puny sword at the mysterious creature. But the blade never connected. Instead, the Thing grabbed his arm and squeezed, sending a loud snap through the air! He fell to his knees, desperately clutching his forearm only held together by shirt and flesh.

"B-beast!" he managed, "M-m-monster!" Then he turned to Milo and huffed, "Run lassy!"

The Thing lurched its head towards the boy, as if finally noticing him. But soon the bandit's fumbling vowels renewed attention. A second later and the Creature gripped the man's face at the mouth and he mumbled something before a muffled CRUNCH silenced him forever.

His partners gone, the Fat Bandit tried to run. But the Beasts' second axe spun through the air, embedding itself in the man's spine. There was a brief yelp, then a heavy thud, and he collapsed beside the boy.

Milo watched, mortified, as the bandit's eyes went cold and one final breath left his lungs.

The Creature's movement startled the boy once more and Milo spun just in time to see the Thing pull it's axe from the first corpse. As it stepped out from the shadows he was able to get a glimpse of what the Thing looked like: it was massive, standing what had to have been at least eight feet tall. There was muscle atop muscle, a body forged from hunting, fighting and God knows what else. Its limbs were long and huge, athletic and chiseled, and at each end were giant feet and hands with equally humongous digits. Strangest most was its rich, green skin, unblemished save for some crude, tribalistic tattoos on its biceps. Finally, it struck the boy - it was an Orc!

In horror and awe, Milo crab-walked backwards until he hit a tree. Trying to stay still and silent, he pressed his body hard against the bark as much as he was able. He hoped, however futilely, that the Orc could only see him if he moved, or at least not find him as appealing as the bandits.

But that hope was shattered when the Creature noticed and began slowly walking through the moonlight towards him. It was barefoot, and its huge feet sent slight tremors through the ground as it lumbered over. Thoom. THOOM. THOOM!

Milo's heart raced. The Thing made his pulse thunder harder than any bandit. *This was it*, he thought! *This was the end…*

But when the shadow overtook him, when all he could see was the gleam in the Orc's eyes and the sheen of blood on its weapons, it stopped short just a few feet away. Pulling its other axe from the Fat Bandit, the Beast stood there, silent and ominous, staring down at the boy as if presenting itself to him, letting him inspect what the three dead men fought.

Milo's eyes had not deceived him. It was indeed an Orc. A rather large one at that. And even more astonishing was that it was no doubt a female! While many might say it was hard to tell Orc genders apart, Milo immediately noticed the astute femininity of the creature. Over eight feet tall, broad shouldered and packed with muscle, but she was definitely a she!

It was her pair of massive, barely covered breasts that first caught Milo's attention. It would have been impossible for any man or boy not to! They were positively exquisite! Her exposed midsection, thick with rippling abs, was relatively thin and tapered yet flared out on either end to frame her hefty tits and shapely hips for a beautiful hourglass figure despite her bulky build. All of her assets were barely covered, whether by purpose or accessibility, and all she wore was a tattered tube top and long, thin loincloth that only covered her groin, held up by a string of stained twine.

Her hair was similarly feminine. It was long and jet black. It looked like it was in a constant state of wetness, probably due to oils and lack of proper cleaning. It hung over her eyes and face, sadly hiding a surprisingly tender appearance. True she shared the pointed ears and sharp tusks as her kin, but perhaps because she was female they were far less extreme. Instead her large lips encased only slight tusks and her ears were thin and almost-elegant, like an Elves.

The She-Orc stared at Milo, her expression curious but indifferent. Her eyes mulled over his body, looking over him as if she was eyeing a steak before dinner.

Milo stared back into the gaze of his brutish savior, the sheer menace that she exuded causing him to shake and tremble uncontrollably. And yet, her strange, alien facial features awoke some other feeling inside him. Sure, she had a mean, unsympathetic resting face. Sure, she had a vicious pair of tusks emerging from her strong lower jaw. And sure, the stare of her yellow, glowing irises seemed intense enough to burn through flesh. But still, in an animalistic, foreign kind of way, she was… attractive.

Strange for a hormonal, teenage boy, Milo was not necessarily sexually active. He had never looked upon women or men with much consideration. But there was something about the Orc that made his heart flutter with newfound effect. The boy wet his mouth and gulped hard, still unsure if the Orc had truly come to his rescue or if he was about to become her fourth victim.

"I-I… umm… th-thank you…" Milo stammered.

She looked back at him for a brief moment, as if surprised he could speak. Then she knelt, sniffed the air around him and grunted.

"What name?" the green amazon growled back in a bassy but feminine timbre.

"M-Milo. My name's Milo..."

She blinked then stared for another moment, before wordlessly leaning in, making the boy whimper and recoil. His heart beat faster and he shut his eyes, expecting the worst.

The intense heat emanating from the Orc was impossible to ignore, as was her hot breath. It didn't stink, Milo thought to himself, and neither did she, which was surprising. Instead she had a thick, fleshy scent mixed with a somehow sweet, pleasant odor of sweat.

When no attack came Milo cautiously opened his eyes. The Orc was only a few inches away from him, her wide nostrils flaring as she sniffed him again and again, moving from neck to cheek, cheek to lips, lips to hair.

Her thick green lips parted, after which a series of incomprehensible words were spoken. *Orcish*, a tongue Milo had never heard before, and it sounded every bit as savage as he had heard described, as if made to instill fear in the other species of the world.

"Ruku," she continued. The deep bass in her voice quaked, penetrating the timid boy to his core. But unlike some of the more masculine guardsmen he had heard in the city, her voice was far more refined. There was a gentle, womanly softness to it, somehow making for a sound that walked a line between intimidating and comforting.

"Rookoo?" Milo attempted, trying to ascertain the bizarre language. "I'm sorry, I don't-"

"No. Ruku name. You Milo. Me Ruku." She said, speaking as if she was talking to a child trying to learn its first words.

"Oh!" Milo beamed. "Ruku! Okay. P-pleased to meet you!" Milo's cheeks reddened, afraid at what his mistake may cost him.

Then with fluid grace the busty Orc rose to her feet and said, "Stand."

Milo cast a glance at the leering face staring down at him, realizing that any resistance may be a gamble on his life. Reluctantly, he stood up on wobbly legs, his back still against the oak tree, clutching the rough bark with delicate fingertips. Once standing, Ruku looked him over again and a silent exchange began, her with an unwavering stare, while his was anxious and worried. She towered over him, almost doubling his height. He was a slight boy, standing barely four foot and eight inches, partially why he was often mistaken for a girl. But now compared to Ruku, he appeared ever smaller in stature.

Suddenly the sizable Orc reached out and wrapped both hands around the boy's midsection, easily grasping the entire circumference of his thin waist. Just as effortlessly as she had dispatched the bandits, Ruku lifted him into the air and gently slung him over her shoulder, belly first, as if he were a sack of flour.

"Hey!" Milo yelped, looking around in a panic, realizing he was being taken. Ruku didn't falter, instead heading for the treeline and away from the city.

He considered screaming louder or perhaps fighting back. But then he looked around the clearing, seeing the broken remains of the three men the She-Orc had just butchered, and caught himself.

"You quiet now, girl," Ruku commanded dryly.

Milo obeyed, not wanting to upset the beautiful yet intimidating warrior.

And with that, the pair vanished into the dark brush of the forest...

By all accounts, Milo was a peasant boy. The youngest of five children and also the runt, Milo was always teased by his three brothers and two sisters for being short, skinny, and girly. He was not strong enough to learn to fight and his skin was too fair to work in the fields, so he was never truly able to give back to his family. One day years ago, he had borrowed a pair of his sisters' clothing to go into town. But somewhere along the way, he lost the five copper pieces given by his mother for a loaf of bread. Ashamed and fearful of the repercussions, he wept in the streets where the merchants normally set up shop.

More often than not, boys are shooed away by the guards as most are orphans or thieving ruffians. But remarkably, the bread merchant took pity on young Milo, thinking he was a girl because of his sisters' ratty dress. So instead of being chased off, Milo was given two loaves of bread and a jug of milk, and in exchange all the vendors asked for was a 'smile from a pretty girl'. He obliged, and ever since, Milo dressed as a girl anytime he went into town.

As he grew older, Milo remained ignorant of most threats outside the city walls. And during his eighteen years, he never once bothered himself with anything but being 'pretty'. He may have been able to list a few other species aside from the Orcs, like minotaurs, trolls or goblins, but other than the fact that they existed, his knowledge was scant. What he did know about Orcs however, was their penchant for violence and bloodshed. They were fierce and cunning, but brutal and widely feared by the town guards. He wasn't sure about much else though, and quite frankly, he didn't really care, as they were something that he never imagined would impact his life in any way.

That is until now....

Deeper into the dense forest they trekked and soon all vestiges of civilization were gone. It was nothing but wilderness in every direction. When Milo realized that even if he did escape, he would have no idea where to go, he began to sob. He regretted ever sneaking through the wall. He wished he never put on this stupid dress. And he certainly bemoaned not listening more intently to all the stories about orcs.

As he bobbed up and down on his captors shoulder, Milo finally spoke up. "Ruku?" he said sniffling, "Where... where are you taking me?"

Before he could even finish his sentence, a giant green hand slapped Milo across his plump rear-end. He squeeked, jumping at the strike.

"Keep quiet," Ruku ordered. "Or I punish."

Milo silenced his gibbering, trying to still his quivering lower lip. With a shudder, he gulped, swallowing what fear and pain he could. He had never been struck like that before. And whether it was the Orcs somewhat feminine touch or the act itself, her slap made a tingle slither through his entire body.

"You understand?" she added.

"... Yes," Milo mumbled.

As they continued, Ruku brought her hand back up to Milo's fleshy backside, squeezing either ass cheek with her large, green mitt. When she was done with his butt she moved to his thick thighs, squeezing as she went as if tenderizing meat.

Milo's cheeks flushed. He had seen girls in the city being groped by horny men but never once thought he'd be on the receiving end. His ass still stung from being hit and he didn't want to admit it, but Ruku squeezing and fondling his butt actually felt nice.

So he kept quiet, bouncing up and down from Ruku's determined strides. He felt like nothing more than a piece of luggage and wanted to struggle or object, but feared any actions would only result in retaliation from his new... owner.

His only comfort was the intense warmth radiating off Ruku's thick skin, keeping the midnight chills at bay. Her scent too also put him at ease though Milo could not fathom why. The strong smell oozing off her sweaty body only heightened as they traveled. It must have been the result of days, perhaps even weeks of not washing, and yet she didn't exactly *look* dirty, with the exception of a few stains of fresh bandit blood.

Much like her brutish, yet alluring looks, there was something intoxicating about the way Ruku smelled. The three dirty bandits had all stank but that was way different, more akin to a sour, rancid, body odor. Hers on the other hand was a concentration of pure, sweaty musk, pungent yet somehow sweet, and perfectly reflected in her looks in the sense that it had both male and female qualities. It was an essence that one might wrinkle your nose at first, only to curiously sniff it again moments later, which was exactly what Milo now found himself doing.

Smelling her was only to distract him from what was going on, Milo told himself. For every second that passed he was taken further away from his home, completely powerless to stop it from happening.

Before long he could see a light, emanating from within the forest with an orange glow. Milo's first instinct was to speak or to ask about it, but he remembered the swift strike to his backside and reconsidered. Ruku moved onward, and as they passed a line of huge oak trees, they emerged inside a small clearing.

Just as effortlessly as she had picked him up, Ruku pulled Milo off her shoulder and sat him on the ground. He spun around immediately, taking in the entire campsite as quickly as possible. Encircled by several worn logs was a bonfire still thriving and crackling as if never left unattended. Behind the logs, which seemed to serve as seats, was a large hide tent with various beddings or blankets inside.

"I here when hear you scream," Ruku said, pointing to the stump she must have been sitting on. Taking her two axes off her waist, she walked past him and set them by the tent, then plopped down onto the same log.

Milo fidgeted in place, still looking and milling about. They couldn't have been more than a few miles from the city, so it wasn't unreasonable that a path or a trail might be nearby. But there were only trees as far as the eye could see.

Ruku noticed his fleeting searching.

"No one out there. No human. We deep in the woods now. You sit." She said bluntly.

Milo swallowed hard and slowly moved to the log beside hers. He watched the Orc stoke the flame with a stick, trying to gauge her expression. Beautiful as she was, she almost looked… sad. Clearing his throat, he scooted closer to her and asked, "are you here alone? All by yourself?"

Ruku snorted as if holding back a laugh.

"Yes. I alone."

"What? Why?" Milo pleaded sympathetically.

"Other Orc no like Ruku. Ruku different." She replied.

That she definitely was, Milo thought. He'd never met an Orc before, but no stories or paintings ever described one as gorgeous and well endowed as she.

"I'm… sorry, Ruku. I know what it's like to be different too."

"Silly human girl. We just spread out," she said, "You meet other Orcs tomorrow."

Great, Milo thought to himself. More Orcs. He wondered how similar they would be to Ruku… What if they all were as large as her? Were they all as attractive as her? And what did she mean by 'being different?'

"So… What are you doing out here?" he continued.

"Ruku scout. Look for human."

Milo frowned at her, before turning his gaze to the flames in front of him. "Humans… like me?"

She nodded. "Yes. Human women good for breeding."

Milo's blood turned to ice.

"W-what?" He sputtered out.

But Ruku didn't answer. Milo felt his heart sink. His suspicions were confirmed. Just like most people back in the city and just like the bandits, the Orc must have thought that he was a girl. Though normally this wouldn't bother the boy, in fact it may have flattered him, but in his current predicament it was doing him a tremendous disservice. Why else would she have taken him? If the Orc had thought he was a boy she probably would have just killed him.

Regardless, he couldn't be turned into breeding stock. He had to say something!

"But Ruku..." Milo began timidly. "I'm… not a girl."

The Orc woman looked up from the fire with certainty and accusation. "You lie. I smell. You girl."

Milo diverted his eyes from her gaze. "But I'm… not, Ruku. Honest." Whatever fate she and the rest of the Orcs might have for him had to be a reprieve. A bargaining chip for the King? Manual labor at some Orcish stronghold? Even servitude sounded more appealing, but at the same time none of them seemed likely. What kind of slave worker could she possibly expect a little girly boy like him to amount to? If he couldn't work in a human town, what good would he be in the Orc Badlands?

Ruku narrowed her gaze, scrutinizing him. "You very pretty girl. I like. Other Orc will like too."

Milo watched her eyes wander. He tried to cover more of his legs with his dress but it had become torn and shredded by the nights' events. When his attempts failed he blushed a deep red, managing to look even more feminine than he already did. He most certainly was a pretty boy, even *he* knew that. But now his crossdressing escapades had turned on him. They may even spell his doom.

Ultimately, he decided not to think about things any further. He was smart. And she was just a big dumb Orc. He had to use his brains to his advantage! Yes! That was it. Surely he could talk himself out of the situation!

"Ruku?" The boy chimed, "please let me go home..." he begged. "My mother is waiting for me..."

"No," she said. "You mine now."

"Yours? I'm not-" He hardly had time to finish his sentence before he felt a big, rough hand suddenly grab his chin, turning his face back to hers. She squeezed his cheeks, forcing his pink lips outward in a forced 'pout'.

"Oww, you're hurting me!" Milo whimpered.

"You mine human girl!" she seethed, feeling her pet squirm as she applied more pressure with her strong fingers.

Tears welled up in Milo's eyes. "Okay. Okay, I-I'm sorry!" he cried, wincing at the ever tightening grip. "I'm... I'm yours."

Ruku smiled slightly and muttered something in Orcish before letting him go, her eyes still affixed to him. "Yes. Good."

Milo rubbed his red cheeks, sulking. "I may be pretty. But I can't give birth, you know..." He said, reluctant but determined.

"What you mean?" Ruku huffed, throwing another piece of wood into the flames. "You can mate with human, yes? Make more for Orcs?"

"No, well... yes. But that's not what I mean!" In a way, she wasn't wrong. Is that what she meant this whole time? It only made sense for them to breed humans, right? Slaves or not. It would have been easier than kidnapping them all the time. But was that truly her plan? To use him as breeding stock with other human women?!

"You make babies." Ruku snapped back at him. "Make for orcs." With her point across she went back to tending the fire and muttered, "Stupid girl."

Milo clenched his teeth in frustration. Did she really just call *him* stupid? A dumb Orc? Just because he was a bit ignorant about the ways of their species, didn't mean that he was slow in any way. In his mind there was no doubt that he could outsmart a big, idiotic barbarian like her. She had him beat in strength and size for sure, but intelligence? Absolutely not!

"Stupid?!" he upstarted.

But Ruku snapped back at him and quickly leaned in to snarl, "QUIET!"

Milo shrank immediately, cowering at her sudden anger. He couldn't help but look away, instead directing his stare into the fire to hide his shame. He truly was just a breeding slave to his captor. Nothing but a tool apparently meant to pass on his unusual, feminine looks to future daughters, only for them to bear orcish children.

After a long silence between them, Ruku sighed. "What you mean 'no give birth'? 'My-low' human girl name?"

Slowly, Milo looked back to her, shame and fear in his eyes. Reluctant to speak, it took him another moment to clear the lump in his throat, straighten up and reply. "No. Milo is a boy's name. And I can't give birth because I'm a boy."

"Boy?" Ruku said, suddenly confused. "You no girl?"

Milo shook his head, his face turning an even deeper shade of red. "No…"

Ruku squinted at him again. "Prove you boy."

"W-what?!" Milo exclaimed, eyes wide. "No! Absolutely not!"

Ruku's expression shifted to anger once again. Her brow furrowed and she grunted. "Prove you boy or I do myself!"

Vivid thoughts of how the Orc intended to do so flooded Milo's brain. Images of his bloody, beaten body ran wild. It felt as if his heart stopped beating from shock alone. Just as Ruku moved to stand he held out his hands to stop her-

"Okay!" he blurted, holding out his hands. "Okay…"

Milo tried to think of any and all ways he could prove his gender. But all save for one seemed would be enough to appease the hulking amazon. Slowly he stood, clutching his dress, and moving towards the bonfire's light he turned and faced the waiting Beast.

Tears twinkled at the corners of his eyes as Milo's fingertips found the hem of his tattered dress. He had to look away, certainly when Ruku leaned in, putting her face only inches from his groin, but most definitely when he swiftly lifted the cloth to show his naked bottom half.

Panties and underwear were a luxury in his village. And even when his family had procured some they had gone to his sisters. So now, bathed in the amber glow of an Orcish bonfire, Milo displayed his small, flaccid dick and tiny ballsack. Smooth and hairless from his cursed genetics, he shivered as the cool night air hit his nethers. He felt a tingle in his tiny boyhood, an embarrassing excitement from merely exposing it. But it was all he could do.

After what felt like entire minutes, Milo let his dress fall back down past his knees. The tears that brewed streamed down his cheeks and he bit his lip to stop it from trembling.

Ruku straightened her back, leaning back on the log. She muttered something in Orcish then looked

at Milo until he turned his head to look back. She delved into the boy's cute, worried eyes, enjoying the shame he exuded.

"Hmph. You right. You no girl."

Milo's tears continued.

"But you no boy either. Not with that small thing."

Mortified is just a word. But a complete and total psychological demeaning of little Milo may have been a better description. Not only was he dressed like a girl, but he looked like one too. And not only was he forced to expose himself to a brutish Orc, but she just scoffed and laughed at his miniscule penis.

He wanted to burst into tears. To let out all the pain and shamefulness. To run crying into the pitch black of night and never be seen or heard from again. Until-

"Come. Sit." Ruku said with her soft but hard tone.

Milo sniffled, instinctively following her command. When he was upon her, he squatted, sitting on her right thigh. Instantly he felt her hands on him and once again found himself intoxicated by her musky scent. Her big, warm hands found him quickly, one on his leg and the other around his waist. They felt nice and for a second he felt comforted. Yet slowly they moved, gradually exploring further… one up his bare calf… the other down to his ass…

Milo couldn't explain it. It was the same tingling he felt when Ruku had struck him. Only now that feeling was radiating all over his body. Anywhere she touched. It was as if her fingertips were charged with lightning.

"Ruku…" Milo whispered. But she continued, silently enjoying the boy's subtle but futile attempt at resistance.

His mind hazy, the boy crooned his neck at the amazon's touch. Her fingers moved up his backside to his neck, turning it to jelly. And that's when he saw it. Between Ruku's legs, her loincloth stood out at a ninety degree angle. His jaw dropped at the hefty appendage jutting out from the Orc 'womans' groin. Beneath the thin loincloth was a bulge so big that it looked as if she had three legs. In fact, it was so moist and swollen he could dinstively see the outline and impression of her massive cock beneath the cloth.

"You still human girl to me, My-low." Ruku whispered in her gruff, seductive tone.

Milo looked up his captor in disbelief. "Oh no, please… I've never done anything like that before," he whimpered, squirming on her lap, his eyes quivering in their sockets.

"Good," Ruku purred, in a new, satisfied tone. "No run. You mine now." With that, she slid a hand under his ass, prodding his crack with a finger. He didn't realize it, but as she did he moaned. A soft, effeminate moan that shuddered off his lips. Then before he could snap back to reality, she lifted him to his feet, spreading her legs so that her barely covered cock hung between them. "Take off clothes, human girl."

Milo stood, cowering. "But-"

"Now!" Ruku snarled!

He should have known that it was pointless to even try...

Swallowing both his pride and fear, Milo began untying his black corset, his trembling fingers clumsily undoing the knots over his abdomen, all while Ruku impatiently watched. Soon enough he was free of it, and let it fall to his feet before moving onto the dress. But just as he was about to slide down his dress' shoulder straps, Ruku grabbed him by the wrists, stopping him from going further.

"I help." Her tone was strangely soothing this time around, as if she could tell that he was embarrassed to undress in front of her.

"O-okay..." Milo mumbled back, letting his arms hang by his sides as Ruku slid the straps over his shoulders. He saw her tent-like loincloth twitch, her barely covered rod just a few inches away from him. He was so hypnotically captivated by the sheer length and thickness of her meat that he barely registered that she had pulled the dress down, exposing his pink, puffy nipples. They were stiff and succulent, perched atop a small budding pair of breasts. They had always been sensitive but when the cold night wind licked them, they sprung to life and aroused an all new euphoria in the boy.

Before long his entire torso was out of the dress, and Milo instinctively tried to cover his nipples with his hands but the big She-Orc smacked them away. He felt naked and preyed upon, as if a hundred onlookers were each watching the act unfold.

Ruku licked her fat lips at the boy's gorgeous body. Just like that face of his, the rest of him oozed with pure sex, as if the goddesses had worked together to mold and form him into the specific artifact of her desire. He had slight, narrow shoulders, a thin waist despite wide, curvy hips and hairless and pristine porcelain-like skin from top to bottom.

The Orc leaned in and licked Milo's taut left nipple, sending a shiver through his lithe, teenage frame. Then before he could gasp again she planted her mouth on his right, taking the whole breast into her toothy maw.

Milo shuddered, feeling his puny dick twitch and stiffen beneath his dress. It rubbed against the silky fabric, sending even more sensations through his receptors. With a loud, wet SMACK the Orc freed his nipple, letting it wiggle slightly before coming to rest on again on his perfect chest.

"Turn around human girl," Ruku commanded, a slight slur in her words caused by her salivating. The boy looked at her with worry in his eyes for a moment, but obeyed. He understood that the Orc was in charge, and that there was no point in trying to resist her.

Slowly Milo pivoted and Ruku devoured his sexy backside, noticing how the dress had bunched up around his wide hips, unable to fall without intervention. She rubbed at the dimples on his back, then thumbed the clothing so that the crack of his shapely ass peeked out.

The wait was over. With breathing heavy, Ruku licked her lips then said, "bend over."

Without a word, and only a hint of hesitation left in him, Milo set his hands down onto the log in front of him and bent forward. His tears returned, and his thoughts deviated just briefly to wonder why he, a man, would be so prone to crying...

Though, not wishing to upset his capture, Milo braced the log, presenting his butt to the horny Orc, thankfully still covered in the bunched up dress. But not for long.

Gradually as to savor the sight, Ruku continued, sliding the dress all the way down his legs until it hit the ground, all while Milo quietly wept.

Just like she had expected, even his ass was perfect. Like the juiciest apple ever conceived, Ruku was in awe at just how disproportionately big, buxom and round it was on that small frame of his. It was an overly plump and mouth watering genetic marvel. An absolute anomaly straight out of some sin conjured by Mother Nature. From where Ruku sat, there was nothing to hint that the legs and ass in front of her belonged to a boy. It was the sexiest, most titillating thing she had ever seen.

Ruku smirked in satisfaction as she reached out to gently touch the smooth surface of his cheeks. Her burly, rough fingers sank into the pillowy flesh much like they would with a pair of soft breasts. When just one finger wasn't enough, she began squeezing and massaging the boy's ass before leaning in to smell his sweet flesh, wanting him to feel her hot breath on his backside. Finally, after touch and scent and smell were almost too much, she spread the ample cheeks apart, revealing Milo's tiny pink hole that was made - no, destined to serve orcish cocks.

With zero hesitation, Ruku gripped the boy by his meaty thighs and spread his ass apart with either thumb, soaking in the beautiful, virgin hole.

As Milo felt the cold night air brush his exposed asshole, he couldn't stop himself from letting out another hushed, girly moan. But that moan would turn into a sharp gasp when the sudden sensation of Ruku's thick, wet tongue dove into his anus. It was a mix of sheer panic and insurmountable pleasure. He could feel her twirling and swirling it around inside him, starting first with just the tip until he opened up more for her. Soon it felt like entire inches were inside him, and he remembered how Orcs had been long theorized to have larger and longer tongues than men. Milo's body reacted on its own, opening his boypussy to invite and accommodate the lustful intruder, beginning the process of stretching him out for the inevitable sodomy.

Ruku continued to batter his hole with her tongue, feeling him slowly relaxing more and more, turning the boy's gasping into loud moans of pleasure. When she had her entire tongue buried, she wrapped her lips around his exit, sucking and slathering him with her orcish saliva inside and out. It was a bit difficult to eat him out properly with her tusks pressed against his thick buttcheeks, but years of practice gave her an edge.

Milo stood there, shivering with pleasure, trying not to make audible noises that gave away how good it all felt. He had never experienced something like this before. He had hardly even masturbated. Each time he tried had always ended in shame. Even now, whilst having a brutish, amazonian Orc eat his asshole without abandon, the deep shame only multiplied. It was as if he was betraying the human race. Instead of being brave and strong, he represented the weakest and most submissive of his kind. But in that moment, whatever and shame Milo felt was vastly outweighed by the intense, carnal pleasure.

After one last long, twirling slathering, Ruku retracted her tongue and squeezed the young boy's voluptuous ass with both hands. She spread his cheeks, opening his drool-soaked cavity as much as virginly possible. Milo gasped, first at the slick sensation of the Orc tongue leaving his hole, and then at the night air hitting his intestines. He felt empty without her hot, wet muscle inside him, and he whimpered at the guilt of enjoying it.

Ruku grunted. "Good meat," she said, using one of her bulky thumbs to pull his pussy lips open wider.

Her words reminded him of the farmers in the city, and how they would often refer to their cattle in a similar manner. Is that truly what he was? Breeding stock? The notion now intrigued him now that he knew what pleasure could come from it.

"Are you gonna... umm... use it now?"

"Yes," Ruku replied, "Soon."

"W-what? Wait, I-" Mylo said, his bottom lip quivering in fear. "No, please don't..."

"Keep quiet," Ruku huffed. "Spread legs."

Milo complied then looked behind him, face red and ran with tears. He saw Ruku still staring at his ass. Then she popped her thumb in her mouth, coating it with saliva. A second later and he felt her pull his buttcheeks apart again, then a broad pressure at his wet orifice.

"OH!" he helped, before the Orc gave his ass another hard SLAP! He bolted up, but found he was held in place by a chunky thumb in his butthole.

Milo stood still bent at the waist, legs spread apart, sweating and panting, squirming from the strange, searing pain Ruku was inflicting. As she sank her digit to its base, his leg trembled and convulsed, like a dog being scratched in the perfect spot. His mind went blank, he couldn't believe that this was reality. He really had been reduced to a sex-slave... for a dumb, stupid Orc. Perhaps multiple ones.

"Mmph," Ruku huffed, "Good. Tight human girl."

"Please... it hurts..." was all the boy had time to utter before the Orc suddenly stood, putting him within inches of that massive thing between her legs. Her loincloth covered cock grazed his legs and ass as she did, sending a shiver through his spine.

Ruku pushed him down, his frail body crumbling. After he dropped she pushed him with her foot, like a light kick, spinning him so he was facing her crotch.

The scent that her body had been constantly emitting washed over him again, only this time with a hundred times the intensity. There was a new, stronger smell that enveloped the camp. It was Orcish cock-musk, seeping out from under Ruku's wet loincloth.

"Cry more, human girl. I like when human beg," Ruku taunted, her hands on her hips, her massive, ample chest standing out like a shelf. "Now you suck or I make you."

Milo swallowed hard, wide eyed at the bulge pressed against the fabric. The thing was barely covered it at all, hanging just behind the loincloth that stopped just past her knees. It twitched every so often, sending a shiver through Milo and the linen. Nevertheless, he moved to his knees with a heart pounding like never before, mostly in fear, but somewhere deep within there was a faint hint of curiosity.

Young Milo would not stay curious for long.

Another phallic twitch and the loincloth slid to one side, unveiling her massive cock to the boy and the cool night air. It hung to her knees and it wasn't even fully hard, drooping slightly from its girthy weight. Milo's facial expression was almost completely blank, and yet within his stunned, wide eyes was indescribable awe. He had never seen one so big. Not like he had ever seen more than a few in his life. But Ruku's mammoth cock was somehow beautiful. Instantly he wanted it in any way he could. It was just as gorgeous as she was and in the chilly night air, he could literally see steam coming off of it.

The thing hanging in front of his face was nothing short of an absolute monster. He couldn't believe his eyes! Starting at the base he traveled down, feeling as if he would never reach the end, but finally arriving at her thick, dark-green glans half covered in skin that was a shade lighter in color. It still swung back and forth slightly, although it was clear that it was engorging, quickly filling up with blood despite its outrageous heft. It didn't take long for it to reach its full size, jutting out straight from Ruku's chiseled body.

Milo was having trouble soaking it all in. Her monster phallus, the dark patch of oily black pubic hair at its base, her smooth skin, her sharp hip bones and most notably the massive softball-sized testes hanging low behind her swollen shaft.

Her size was not the most overwhelming aspect of it all. Now that her penis was free, its smell was even stronger, invading Milo's nostrils with its unique, pungent, intoxicating scent. Breathing through his mouth only worsened his desire, as the fleshy, musky odor only made his mouth water.

"Hmph," Ruku chuckled, half-grunt and half-laugh. "You humans all same."

Milo shook his head in an attempt to conjure up a reply. "Huh? Uh... wha...?" he slurred, the masculine scent of the orc-cock practically melting his brain.

She chuckled at his dumb, drooling facial expression. "No human girl can resist."

He wanted to protest. To refute her. To prove somehow he wasn't utterly enthralled. But Milo couldn't think straight. He was so incredibly... and insatiably... horny. And each new lungfull of musk only drove his body more and more into overdrive.

"See? All human girls meant to be slaves. You no different."

As much as he would like to lash out at her, all he could do in the moment was pant like a bitch in heat, his eyes glued to the huge, green, She-Orc cock in front of him. He cursed himself internally. Why was it so hard to resist it? The smell was disgusting... for the most part at least... And the size... The whole thing was well over a foot in length, thick as his forearm, and covered in huge, pulsating veins.

"Here, I show you." It was then Ruku ran out of patience. In a flash, she grabbed a fistful of Milo's wavy, auburn hair and yanked his face to her crotch, pressing his nose against her wet piss-slit.

Milo almost fainted at the concentrated dose of Orc-stench. And the dollop of pre-cum that had emerged smeared over his nose and lips as Ruku held him in place. Despite how much he would have denied it, he had never been more turned on in his life. He could literally hear his heartbeat in his ears, feel the tingling shiver through his body and his comparatively tiny penis instantly go rock hard, leaking sweet pre-cum of his own.

Before he could cognitively react, he instinctively parted his trembling lips and opened his mouth, instantly pressing his mouth to the swollen, green cockhead. It was big. So big that his tiny mouth seemed to have no hope of swallowing it, instead just planted on the tip like a suction cup. Mouth agape and mashed against the phallus, Milo's tongue reached out to take its first taste of Orc pre-cum.

"Ooh," Ruku moaned at the sudden tickle on the tip of her cock. "Good girl. Good slave..."

She relaxed her grip and instead ran her rough fingers through the soft hair of her fellator, as if a reward for not having to give instructions. Then, he surprised her once again, as he continued to not only lick her slit, but the entire surface of her exposed cockhead, twirling his tongue round and round, smearing pre-cum and saliva alike.

The salty, savory taste of the mix was a far stronger flavor than he could have ever have anticipated, but not a bad one by any means. The musk clouded his mind as all his senses honed in on the act and task at hand.

"Do same with these..." Ruku purred, lifting her shaft away from Milo's still moving tongue. He let out a small whimper as she did, leaving a single spindle of saliva that trailed from his lips to her moist head.

Confused, Milo looked up at her as his worshipping was interrupted, but before him, just as prevalent as her cock, was a pair of huge, smooth, green balls. As sizable as softballs and more than his hands could ever hope to hold, hanging halfway down her thighs, the two testes rested, glistening with slick Orc-sweat.

They almost seemed the source of the vicious smell. And that pungent odor filled Milo with just one emotion: Lust.

As he looked at them, he couldn't help but think how absolutely beautiful they were. Their size, roundness, smoothness, their shiny, dark-green surface... And he wanted nothing more but to taste them.

Milo slid forward on his knees, until he could feel the heat radiate from Ruku's hefty, gargantuan balls onto his face, pausing for a second to inhale one last whiff. With trembling fingers he reached out to hold them with his palms, the warm, copious sweat they were coated in instantly transferred to his hands and began running through his fingers and down his forearms. He shuddered as he lifted them up, in awe of how heavy they were.

Sticking out his tongue, he craned downward, immediately suckling their surface like a complete degenerate, lapping up as much of their salty flavor as he could. He licked with purpose, his nose wedged in the flesh between her nuts while holding them tightly against his cheeks, taking deep whiffs of her delicious smell and the sweat that quickly coated his face.

What on Earth am I doing? Milo thought. But he couldn't stop himself.

There he was, face full of fat Orc balls, his eager mouth licking and sucking the sweat off them, while an equally fat cock rested on top of his head. Deep down Milo was screaming at himself to stop, that he was a proud human, that he was a man and not a slave girl. But he couldn't bring himself to let up. He kept on sniffing, licking, sucking, like there was no tomorrow, trying to justify his heinous actions by whatever means he could muster. But every thought was pervaded by the desire to please his captor…

Just when Milo thought the musk couldn't be more invasive, Ruku cupped him by the back of the head and pulled him in tighter, mashing his face, nose and mouth against her testicles.

For a moment, he couldn't breathe, the taste and smell was overwhelming. His eyes rolled back in his head. He murmured something incoherently. And even though he was practically being suffocated, the only thing he could feel or care about, was how his cock twitched then spasmed, spurting cum to the ground.

"Good slut," Ruku said before releasing him.

Free now, Milo gasped, trembling as his first orgasm coursed through his body. He had to hold on to Ruku's thighs just to keep from collapsing.

"Slave girl use mouth now."

"Oh, God… fuck…" Milo moaned, his voice barely audible underneath the massive cock resting on top of his head and the huge balls pressed against his face.

"Shuddup," Ruku commanded abruptly. "And suck Orc cock."

Milo froze, dazed in a state of post orgasm, swiftly overtaken by the new command. He stared up at it, at her, over the arm sized piece of green meat that still glistened with her sweat and his spit.

By now though, he knew not to linger for too long.

Ruku glared at him. "I know you want, human whore."

Milo reached out to grip the hefty cock, salivating from the touch alone, and aligned it with his mouth. His tiny hand looked as if it couldn't move the thing, like a baby's hand trying to move an oak tree. It was so thick around that his tiny digits had no hope of wrapping around its circumference. Yet he moved it with relative ease, driven by strength to do the Orc goddesses bidding. So after pressing it to his nose to give it one long, drawn out sniff, he wrapped his lips around her glans. Miraculously, most of the head fit, perhaps from lubricant or lust or some newfound ability for Milo to unhinge his jaw, and soon his tongue began lapping up every drop of precum Ruku offered. Right away, he could hear the low, throaty moans coming from his captor, and as he looked up at her with big, yellow eyes for her reassurance.

He was not disappointed.

"You want Orc cum?" Ruku whispered.

Milo quickly popped her cock out of his mouth whilst still looking up at her, his cheeks red in embarrassment. "Yes!" he huffed, before returning to his fellatio.

"You will like. All humans do. Sweet like honey…" She ran a calloused, green thumb over his cheek as she spoke in an almost tender, loving fashion. "Weak girl slave like you will love."

Milo felt another trembling course through him. He might cum again from her humiliating words alone. Just what the hell was wrong with him?! Now he was unable to shake the way she had described her semen. Could it really have a sweet flavor? If it was anything like her delicious pre-cum, he definitely wanted to taste it!

With a newfound sense of determination, Milo doubled his efforts in bringing the savage Orc to orgasm. He opened his mouth as far as he could, trying vainly to take the rest of her thick head inside. Finally his tongue could explore more and teased her shafts' immediate underside. He opened so wide it hurt. It felt like his jaw was going to split in two. Yet even when he found himself unable to widen any further, he simply pushed himself forward… downward. Until finally, the entire head was lodged inside his mouth, his teeth stuck behind its rim.

"Oh!" Ruku found herself taken off guard. She moaned, gripping the boy's head with her big hands. "Good slave…"

Despite gagging almost instantly from the tip of her cock pressed against the back of his throat, Milo used his tongue and pouty lips to his best effort, sucking and licking whatever surface he could come into contact with. He felt a rush of more pre-cum and assumed he was doing well. He had only been at it for a few seconds, and he had already been forced to swallow numerous times. Despite his gulping, gallons still poured off his lips. Whether it was his saliva or her juices he did not know, he just kept drinking as much as he could.

"More slutty girl," Ruku purred, applying more pressure to the back of Milo's head. She pulled him down, putting his head, neck and body at a ninety degree angle. "Swallow more…"

With an expression of pure horror, Milo looked up at her pleadingly as she attempted to push her cock deeper. He put his hands against her thighs, trying to indicate that he had hit his limit. Though he knew he did not possess nearly enough strength to make a difference, he had to do *something*. Sure enough, it didn't matter. In the next instant he could feel her cock forcing its way further in, flattening his tongue and tonsils to make room for itself, making Milo cough, gag, then almost retch.

His body froze. His eyes bulged. It pushed past his reflex and down his throat. Ruku growled with ecstasy.

It seemed like an impossible fit, but the boy was a natural cocksleeve. As she descended down his throat he panicked and spasmed, but Ruku held him in place.

Milo's urge to throw had never been stronger, and yet he was no longer even gagging. Perhaps it was a sign that he was about to faint, as soon it seemed like his entire body had given up on even trying to resist her, his arms turned to jelly, his knuckles went white, his eyes rolled back…

When Ruku reached the halfway mark, she was satisfied. The boy had flailed at first but now was limp like a wet noodle, and finally it was time. With another smirk, she started rocking back and forth with her hips, repeatedly pulling out a few inches before immediately plunging them back in the hot, young mouth, moaning each time she drove past his tonsils. *This boy's throat was unreal*, she thought, as not even a minute had passed and she could already feel an orgasm building.

Ruku looked down at her slave, biting her lip as she took in the view. There really was nothing like seeing the look on a human's face as she shoved her massive cock down their throat, their stretched out, pink lips around her dark-green shaft making for the most beautiful contrast imaginable. She could feel her huge, undulating balls practically aching with a need for release, her potent sperm in an uproar to mark the boy forever.

Milo noticed it too. While he may have been close to unconsciousness, he could feel a violent throbbing, stretching his throat out even further, and those low moans coming out of Ruku's mouth had turned into something bestial, almost frightening. He looked up at her past the massive, flopping tits, at the deep lines on her face and the drool hanging off her lips and chin... Yeah, he knew he was about to get fed.

Reaching down, Ruku slapped the boy's juicy, heart-shaped ass, sending ripples through the fleshy orb that seemed to never end. Fucking constantly, she ran a hand down his back and led her middle finger to his hungry hole, plunging it inside. Milo let out a loud squeak, muffled from the foot long Orc phallus down his throat. His puny cock twitched again, shooting a thin rope of cum onto the puddle in the grass he had already formed. Ruku smiled, finding the slippery hole still wet with her superior Orc saliva, so much so that her bulbous finger slid in with relative ease.

Ruku hissed between her teeth as her balls hit their boiling point, her hips pummeling back and forth with ever increasing speed. The boys muffled cries ricocheted off the trees and the wet, sloshing sounds reverberated through the darkness. Her cock violently plunged down her slave's throat again and again, treating him like the little human sex-toy that he was. She could feel him convulsing even harder around her arm-thick shaft as his lungs panicked for air, but it only gave Ruku the last push that she needed, his tight, wet insides had milked her to fruition.

GRRRAAAWWWRRR!!! Ruku roared, howling into the night like an animal. With one last, punishing thrust, impaling the boy slave with three-fourths of her womanhood, she emptied her balls down Milo's esophagus.

It was as if a volcano erupted, jettisoning her hot, thick Orcish cum down Milo's gullet. He swallowed what he could. But his stomach was filled in seconds.

Milo couldn't believe the amount of thick, scalding fluid Ruku was injecting inside him. There was just so... much... cum... and there seemed to be no end in sight. Her cock kept throbbing, spewing more and more semen down his throat, even to the point that he could feel his belly expanding slightly, as if he had stuffed himself with food.

He had never felt as weak as in that moment. The way she held his head in place with her big, strong hands, the way she practically roared with pleasure while he gagged pathetically, the way she looked down at him during her draining orgasm... All while her footlong green cock broke him in for the first time, branding him as nothing more than a slave for a savage Orc.

Suddenly, Ruku unsheathed herself, pushing Milo back down to his knees and grabbing her cock mid shaft, pinching off the bio-organic flow. There was no resistance. The boy's body refused cognitive location. He was her plaything. And while he could see and feel the things happening, he could not stop them. Instinctively he gasped for air and coughed up semen, but could do little else besides sway back and forth on the ground.

"Open mouth!" Ruku grunted, waiting until Milo's most basic motor functions returned and he slowly looked up at her. "Open mouth, human whore!"

He obeyed, opening and sticking his tongue out. When he did, Ruku relaxed her grip, opening her seminal pipeline so that her cock could erupt with another volley of sticky, stinky cum, painting the boy face-first. With mouth agape, rope after rope drenched him, coating his hair, chest and shoulders until nearly all of him was painted white. It covered him in a thick, pudding-like layer, its heat almost scorching his skin. He swallowed what he could, then opened wide again struggling to swallow whatever she managed to land in his mouth. Truth be told, it was hard to even see Milo's facial features anymore with such thick layers covering him. It was definitely a look that suited the boy.

Why...? Milo thought to himself as he gulped another load down. *Why does it have to taste so good*? Ruku was right. It was sweet like honey. And he loved it.

Eventually and finally, Ruku was drained. With a steady trickle still oozing out of her tip, she stood there, even more sweaty than before, looking down at her slave with a satisfied grin on her face.

"Good slave," she praised, her tone calm and soothing, as if her wild temper had died out with her orgasm. She wiped the sweat off her forehead, tucking back the unkempt, black hair that hung across her glistening face, and plopped back down on the log below her.

Mylo barely registered her words. He just sat there, completely drenched, exhausted, and... horny. Really, really horny. His tiny little dick stood straight up, stray orc-cum covering its surface, the mere heat it radiated onto him feeling better than his hands ever had. Hell, he was close to orgasm himself, with no other stimulation than just that. The next thing he knew, Ruku was slipping something over his head. He blinked and shook, then wiped the cum from his eyes so he could see. His vision was blurry but when the thing tightened around his neck, he realized - it was a rope. Not unlike the one holding up Ruku's loincloth, the frayed and dirty twine went snug as she tied around his collar, creating a makeshift 'leash'.

"H-hey… what're you doing?" Milo stammered, tugging at the bind around his slender neck.

"Shuddup slave girl." Ruku said, tugging at the twine so hard that he nearly fell face first into the grass.

"Ow…" Milo yelped, his cheeks burning. His senses and surroundings were becoming clear again. His lust had subsided but fear returned.

Milo's eyes fluttered and closed as he felt himself drifting off, trying to keep a beed on his gargantuan captor. That is, until he felt Ruku swiftly grab his legs and pin them together at the ankles. She had more rope, like the kind around his neck.

"What are you doing now...?" Milo asked weakly, his throat sore and raspy.

Ruku didn't answer. She was too busy tying his ankles.

"Wha... Why are you tying me up?" he mumbled.

"Cause you slave," Ruku said nonchalantly.

Milo sulked. She wasn't wrong. But was she really expecting him to sleep outside like this? Covered head-to-toe in her sticky seed? It was everywhere!. His hair... his face... his body...

She finished her binding then wrapped it around a stake planted in the ground.

"W-wait!," Milo pleaded, "you… you're not going to leave me out here all night are you?"

"Quiet," Ruku huffed.

Milo recoiled again, tugging futility at the rope.

"Sleep now slave girl," Ruku said, "you meet other Orcs tomorrow."

The Orc disappeared into her tent and Milo swallowed hard, an all new fear taking hold at 'meeting' more of her brutish, green-skinned kind the following day.

But then a slight smile crept across his lips...

THE END

SECRET (FUTA) INGREDIENT

For most people, Mondays are the low point of the week. Saturday and Sunday are over with and whatever fun you might have had is replaced by bumbling co-workers, irrational bosses and just work in general. But for Carmella 'Carmen' Mendoza, Monday's were actually something to look forward to. Every weekday was in fact. Because every weekday she would get to go to a job she loved, and each morning she would get to see *him*.

Some might call it a crush. Others, an obsession. But for the past few weeks Carmen had become infatuated with a frequent young customer, Cody. It had been two days since she saw him last, and oh what a painful weekend it had been without being able to gaze upon his sexy, young body. But now, Monday had finally arrived and her eyes would soon be sated.

Monday through Friday Carmen's routine was the same, waking at five, go for a quick jog, shower, then open the café doors at six. As a manager it was her job to get there early, even before the owner, and prepare so the day would run smoothly. Her co-workers wouldn't start work until later, and she liked it that way, so she could make sure everything was perfect before the day really began. But most importantly, she would be the only one in the store when Cody arrived...

"*It was almost time*", Carmen said to herself, "*he'll be here any minute...*"

Using a mirror in the employee breakroom, Carmen looked herself over one last time. Without makeup she would have been a stunning beauty, but she had dolled herself up for the occasion. Carmen was a bronze, six foot tall, latin goddess, with smooth mocha skin, trademark curvy hips, a flat stomach and a full, pert B-Cup bosom. More athletic than busty, but still sultry and curvaceous in ways supermodels would envy. She fluttered her eyelashes and raised her thin eyebrows, the carefully groomed, pitch-black strands perfectly enhancing her tanned, caramel skin. Her hair was an elegant shade of dark brown, straight and perfect, today pulled into a tight ponytail. Beauty aside, her work uniform was all but atrocious. A trademark of the establishment that most are familiar with: white short sleeve shirt, bright orange hot pants and white knee-high socks. Her tight, athletic form was the only thing that made the slutty gettup even the least bit posh.

After pouting her cherry-red lips and blowing herself a kiss in the mirror, Carmen stood, looking around to make sure that everything was in order. Her eyes then fixated at the front doors, eagerly anticipating the moment they would swing open and Cody would enter. Her heart beat faster with each second that ticked away until her inevitable encounter. Though if past experiences were anything to go by, she wouldn't have to wait very long...

Cody stretched his thin, pale arms above his head and let out a long yawn. *He was almost there,* he said to himself, hungry for breakfast. On the edge of the dormitory apartments where he lived, there wasn't a lot to see or do, but one little establishment stood out to him. Café Sirénes, a quaint little place where the staff was nothing but beautiful women and the food was surprisingly tasty. It also helped that it was so close to the dorms, so that each morning as he headed to school, he could easily stop by, grab a bite, then head to class. So, at the same early hour every weekday, Cody would swing by the little café and have breakfast.

He was a slight young thing. More of a boy than a man really. Who was just under five feet tall with a slender form and soft features. His skin was smooth and blemish free and his small, thin waist was a stark contrast to his engorged hips, plump ass and thick thighs. He had been mistaken for a girl more times than he'd like to admit but liked the idea of feeling pretty. And though he tried to dress masculine to deter unwanted looks, Cody often found shopping for clothes that fit him difficult, so he would often have to purchase tomboyish girls clothes just to get something adequate.

Like a beacon of comfort within the dreary streets and buildings, Cody soon spotted the light of his destination beaming out onto the cold, dark surroundings. As much as he loved their breakfast, he hated walking the murky stretch to the café each morning. It scared him. There was no telling what dangers lurked in the shadows, ready to pounce on his supple, young body. Why, just last week he saw a boy being chased by two thugs down an alley! But coming closer to Café Sirénes now, he felt safe and relieved. He could almost feel the warmth reaching out to embrace him, pulling and coaxing him in.

Gingerly, Cody stepped up to the door and swung it open. The familiar sound of the bell ringing overhead and the smell of freshly baked bread immediately made him feel at home. Like always, he expected nothing short of perfection in the food that he would receive, and one glance at the pretty girl behind the counter confirmed his expectations would be met.

God he loved this place.

For almost a month the same girl had been the one to take his orders every time he came in, and she had never disappointed him. Not only was the food that she prepared always perfect, but the glowing smile on her beautiful face was half the pleasure of Café Sirénes. She was everything he looked for in a girl, albeit a bit tall, but something about her athletic figure and height made her exotic and mysterious. Whatever it was, he was fully enamored by the dark-skinned amazon.

Carmen was her name, a tall, latina woman who appeared to be a little older than him, with stunningly good looks and a tight, toned figure. But it wasn't just her appearance that struck young Cody, it was her bubbly, cheerful demeanor. She was the type of girl that always made him feel special whenever he was there, even though he knew that it was common practice for waitresses and employees in her line of work to always flirt with customers, Carmen's kindness seemed genuine.

Trying his best to control the smile on his face, Cody walked up to the counter.

"Hey there! Good morning!" Carmen exclaimed.
"Hi!" Cody said, having to look up to gain eye contact with her since she stood over a foot taller than him.

"Let me guess," Carmen said playfully, "The usual?"

Cody nodded. "You bet," he said, already handing over his debit card.

"Sure do like those scrambled eggs, huh?" Carmen said with a wink. "Okay! Comin' right up!" she beamed.

With a flick of her wrist she slid the card through its reader then held it out for the boy to grab.

"Thank you," Cody replied. As per usual, Carmen didn't merely place the card into his hand, but instead went as far as to rub his palm with her fingers in a long, drawn out exchange. What would normally be a simple hand off was now an exaggerated touching or stroking gesture. It did make him a bit uncomfortable at first, but now he had come to like her soft touch and the smell she left behind. Whatever lotion or soap she used was intoxicating, and sometimes when he could afford it, he would sniff his hand throughout the day.

"No, no. Thank YOU sweetie," Carmen purred, keeping her eyes on Cody as he tucked the card back into his pocket. She looked him over, not hiding her gaze if he were to notice. He was wearing a tight black shirt and equally form-fitting gray shorts. So short in fact that his ass looked like it was eating them and his huge clefts of fleshy cheeks hung out the bottom.

Butterflies began to churn in Cody's stomach. The touch and the compliment from the beautiful woman was almost too much for him to handle. He shot her an awkward smile, trying to hide his nervousness. It wasn't that he disliked the attention in any way; in fact far from it, he just didn't know how to respond to it. He never had. Interactions with the opposite sex had been scarce, especially with one as beautiful and exotic as Carmen. Furthermore, as far as he knew she was all alone during these early hours, so perhaps she was just a bit extra happy to see another person's face.

Whatever her reason, Cody noticed her look him over again then turn and head for the kitchen.

Thinking nothing more of it for the time being, Cody went to sit down at the same corner table he always did. He put his backpack on the floor and looked around the cozy interior, the various light fixtures on the walls and in the ceiling set to a perfect level of brightness that neither hurt one's tired eyes nor made the place gloomy. Faint, upbeat music could be heard from the overhead speakers, setting a nice mood for any groggy customers that might show up before sunrise. Cody closed his eyes and slid further down his chair, the only thing that could make the start of his week any better being the delicious breakfast that he was soon to be devouring.

Out of all the various cafés, fast food restaurants, convenience stores and gas stations he had gone to for quick, cheap meals to start off his school days with, none of them were as good as Café Sirénes. Every meal he had ever had there, even prior to settling on his usual order, had been great, but their scrambled eggs were out of this world. How it was even possible to achieve such intense flavors from such a simple dish was downright mind-boggling.

At first Cody thought the secret lay in the café's recipe, but the few times anyone other than Carmen had prepared it for him proved otherwise. She was the only one able to blow his mind with how delicious it was every time. Even disregarding the perfectly creamy texture, it had this strange flavor that, while hard to place, worked wonders. A hint of sweetness that cut through the mild, buttery flavor one would expect from scrambled eggs. He wondered if it was some sort of family recipe or if Carmen only held the secret. He had considered asking her but never once had the courage.

Cody wondered then, if the delicious breakfast would have the same effect on him as the past few times. A taste so good it literally excited him. At least that was the best way he could describe it. He couldn't fully explain it, and he had never really masturbated with such frequency, but something about those yummy scrambled eggs seemed to light a fire inside him.

Carmen hummed to herself as she picked out the assortment of things for Cody's order. 'The usual' as it came to be called was Café Sirénes scrambled egg plate, which was simply two eggs served with grilled tomatoes and a cream cheese bagel.

Like every time he came by, Cody's image was immediately ingrained into Carmen's mind anew. This time it was a skin-tight, long-sleeved, black compression shirt that covered his flat chest and slim waistline, and a pair of almost equally tight, gray short shorts that hugged his perky bubble-butt and smooth, feminine thighs. True the outfit may not have been the most comfortable for that chilly morning, but Carmen was ecstatic he chose it. He and his frail little body looked absolutely adorable!

Regardless of his clothing, Carmen would have fawned over him anyway, just from his adorable face, with his little up-turned button nose, and the medium-length golden locks of hair that tickled his slender neck and shoulders. Not to mention that smile of his... It made her heart throb without fail.

Just thinking about him made her body temperature rise.

It was time, she thought.

At last, she set the carton of eggs down with the rest of the ingredients on the table, making sure that everything was present. Eggs, cream, salt, pepper, chives, butter, tomatoes... Other than the bagel and a drink that she would procure on the way out, all the things required to make Cody's meal were all in front of her. With the exception of her one, secret ingredient...

The lush booth of Cody's seat was nice and soft against his plump boy-butt. He crossed his arms tightly around himself and rubbed them against the black fabric of his shirt, massaging his smooth, creamy skin underneath. Freshly showered and moisturized, his own soft touch almost drew out an adorable little moan from him; such was the extent of his comfort.

Relishing in his own soft skin and mouth watering at the coming feast, his stomach growled with anticipation. His thoughts meandered but then his body twitched. He had been so eager for breakfast that morning that he hadn't even taken the time to pee.

Letting out a groan, he stood then scanned the café for a restroom. But to his surprise and annoyance he couldn't see one. In fact, his memory raced, he had never seen one there ever! *Surely they must have one somewhere*, Cody thought, baffled at why any restaurant might make their bathroom hard to find.

At the very least there must be one for the employees, right? In the breakroom perhaps? Maybe he could just peek into the kitchen and ask Carmen. She was always so happy and bubbly, he couldn't imagine her upset by his exploratory trespass! Besides, he was more than just another customer by now.

Still looking about as if he somehow missed a restroom somewhere, Cody slowly made his way towards the kitchen at the rear of the café. Pushing the swinging door open slightly he peered inside, expecting to see Carmen hard at work on breakfast, but she was nowhere to be seen.

Curiously he passed through the kitchen towards a back door emblazoned with a placard that said 'Employees Only'. He gave the door a soft knock and waited a few seconds for a response, but none came. He knocked again, a little harder, and again went unheard. While he didn't want to just barge in, it seemed like that was the only way he could go about it.

Pushing down the door handle and carefully cracking the door, Cody peeked inside. It was a breakroom for sure, with a couch and a few tables, but he couldn't see all of it without opening the door wider. What gave him pause was the strange sound coming from the other side. Though faint, he thought he could hear her voice emanating from within. At first he thought it was the television, then perhaps Carmen talking on the phone, but neither sounded right for the muffled 'humming' he heard.

Cautiously and silently he moved, not sure exactly why he was acting so stealthily. As the door opened further, the sounds became clearer, but if they were words they must have been spoken in another language.

Quiet still Cody craned his neck around the door. The sounds were words alright - Spanish. It was Carmen, muttering Spanish in low, hushed whispers.

He pushed the door further, still unable to see the source. The sounds shifted in tone. They almost seemed like... whimpers? Had Carmen gotten hurt? Was she crying?

No. In fact she was far from it.

Looking further inside, Cody's eyes went wide at the sight-

Carmen, the tall, beautiful latina who he had ogled over for weeks, was leaning forward against a small table, legs spread, feverishly stroking a fat, brown, near ten-inch cock that was jutting out of her unbuttoned shorts. In front of her was a table that she was leaning on with one hand, and positioned directly under her wet, bulbous cocktip was a bowl. Beside that, a carton of eggs.

The muffled whimpers that had kept Cody's presence concealed continued uninterrupted as he stood there in shock, watching Carmen, eyes closed and dick gripped tight, masturbating. Her whimpers turned to moans, held back and muffled by the collar of her shirt she had apparently stuffed into her mouth to bite down on. That is, until her teeth suddenly let go and let her voice flew free.

"Mmm, joder, sí mi pequeña zorra... Yesss Cody, baby... Si... Si..." she moaned, throwing her head back.

Cody blushed and felt a shudder go down his spine. Carmen's mix of Spanish was impossible for him to decipher, but there was no doubt about what else she had just uttered. He couldn't believe it! She was masturbating... and thinking of him of all people!

Then Carmen's moans suddenly came out with shorter intervals and greater volume, and she leaned forward over the table...

That's when young Cody understood.

Her long, thick, caramel-colored cock was forcibly angling downwards. Its smooth surface seemed to undulate. Her hand started moving faster and faster until it was nearly a blur, and Carmen directed the tip of her cock into the bowl.

Cody had come just in time to get a perfect view of the fruits of Carmen's labor. It began with her entire body tightening up, quickly followed by a thick spurt of white cum being unleashed into the bowl, hitting its glass bottom with an audible SPLAT. She shuddered a moan. Rope after rope of equally voluminous amounts followed, Carmen's labored huffs unable to drown out the splattering noise of her cum forming a pool inside the basin. With both horror and awe on his face, Cody covered his wide open mouth with his hand as he continued to watch her drawn-out orgasm, every fiber of his being telling him to quietly turn around and head back.

At last, the deranged noises of pleasure pouring out of Carmen's mouth started to die out along with her orgasm. She let out a few last dribbles into the bowl and sighed, her chest and perky breasts heaving up and down while her legs quivered in afterglow.

After having watched in silence for what seemed like an eternity, Cody realized that all Carmen had to do was turn her head slightly to notice him. So, just as quietly as he entered, he began backing out of the room, carefully bringing the door with him. Once back out in the kitchen, he remained still for a moment, in complete disbelief of what he had just witnessed, his heart beating like crazy and his breath close to hyperventilating levels. Then almost as if a sign from the heavens, he saw the restroom just beside the employee breakroom door.

Gulping, he finally managed to make his legs move, shuffling into the small, one-person lavatory and locking the door behind him. Breathing heavy he slammed his back against the door, trying to clear his head. But it was no use. All he could see were vivid images of Carmen's engorged girlcock and the pints of semen she had just unleashed into the now fully decorated bowl. Finally, nature overcame thought and Cody remembered the entire reason he got up from his seat. Rushing to the urinal, he yanked down the front of his shorts allowing his small yet erect penis spring out.

Why was he hard? Was he really that turned on by the sight?

Relieving his bladder seemed to calm his nerves. So after washing his hands and splashing some cold water on his face, he stowed his hard-on and scurried back to his empty booth, scanning his surroundings to make sure Carmen was still absent.

The shock on his face was still very much present, and the images of Carmen's huge cock replayed over and over again in his mind. His calm demeanor from earlier was gone as he sat back down in his chair, trying vainly to rearrange his private parts within his tight-fitting clothing.

He had so many questions: why did Carmen have a dick? Why had she been masturbating in the break room? Why did that somehow turn him on? What was she doing with all those ingredients? What was she doing with that mixing bowl? Why do it when she should have been busy preparing Cody's scrambled eggs...?

"Oh my God..." Cody murmured aloud, quickly clamping his hands over his mouth.

Truth be told it wasn't hard to work out the answers to his questions on his own, but he didn't want to believe the only logical conclusion he could arrive at. The ingredients on the table in front of her; the bowl that had gathered her semen; the odd, but exciting flavor that was unique to the scrambled eggs she had served in the past... There was no doubt about it.

All this time... he had been eating Carmen's cum!

Now, an innocent, girly boy like Cody wasn't exactly great at handling conflict, but he knew that this was a big deal. He knew that it was something that should be reported to the owner immediately.

How many crimes Carmen had committed with her shameful act would probably take a long time to list, but even looking past the moral side of things, this must surely have been a health hazard.

But… he didn't really want to get Carmen in trouble, did he? She had always been so nice to him. Nicer than anyone else he had ever met. In fact he was almost starting to think she might have even liked him.

What am I even still doing here? Run you idiot! Cody thought to himself. *Just get up and leave and never look back!* But still he sat there, unable to will himself to even move. Was he afraid? Did he want to confront her? Or report her? Or was it something else? Was there more to it than that?

Just by looking at him, it wasn't hard to see that Cody wasn't exactly a ladies' man. In fact he had only ever kissed a girl and was still a virgin. Most people assumed that he wasn't even a male to begin with, judging from the way he looked and dressed. He just happened to be 'unfortunate' enough to not only naturally look like a short, flat chested, cute young girl, but also have the fashion sense of one.

Cody's sex drive had never been particularly high either. But like any teenage boy, his thoughts frequently lingered on sex and girls. He had always considered himself straight too, although he never had a girlfriend. But now, the image of Carmen and her throbbing cock made him question everything he thought he knew about himself. He couldn't help it! Even the straightest of men would have had difficulty looking away from the dark-skinned beauty!

Right? Cody asked himself, suddenly breaking into a cold sweat.

Carmen was gorgeous. There was no doubt about that. She had a voluptuous figure, long athletic legs, washboard abs and perky breasts. But all Cody could think about was her veiny, delicious looking cock!.

The time was drawing near. Carmen would be returning any second now.

Cody's chest heaved with each increasingly panicked breath he took. He eyed the kitchen door, waiting still, for reasons unknown, for it to swing open…

"Scrambled eggs, a cream cheese bagel and one cup of orange juice!" Carmen sang out.

She slid the plate over the table, her eyes glued to the boy as always, noticing his cheeks flushed with a slight red hue.

"Is… everything okay?" Carmen asked.

Her words didn't seem to register. Cody just stared down at the luscious, fluffy eggs as they came to rest in front of him.

"Um, Cody? Hun?" She asked again, snapping his attention to her.

"Y-yeah, I'm fine," Cody said. "It's just a bit… warm in here…"

Carmen scanned his girly body. "Well, I can't do much about that… I might've said take off some clothing, but that doesn't look possible for you."

His cheeks took on a new shade of darker red and he looked down at his thick, fleshy thighs. Unbeknownst to Carmen, he still had an erection but thankfully having such a small penis, it wasn't that noticeable.

"I... I think I'll be fine," Cody eventually mustered.

"Ooookay! Well, enjoy! I'll be back in a jiffy!"

Forcing herself to tear her eyes away from the pretty little girly boy, Carmen spun and headed back to the kitchen. Like always, regardless of whether Cody noticed or not, she made sure to pout her ass out as much as possible, swaying her hips with each step. The front of her shorts still strained from her still blood-filled cock, hastily crammed into the confines post-coitus. The thought of Cody once again eating her seed made her pulse rattle. If past instances were anything to go by, no additional customers would come in for quite some time, so she could savor the sight of him consuming her essence.

This was it, Carmen thought to herself. *When he finishes breakfast, I'm going to make my move.*

She had waited long enough. She wanted more. She needed it. There was no way he could resist her charm and her looks. She was going to ask him out before he left. Nothing would stop her now.

Cody's enthusiasm for his usual breakfast was utterly absent. His breaths snapped with anxiety as they took in the deliciously scented plume of steam rising from the pile of creamy eggs. His stomach growled again. He was so hungry... and they looked so amazing. But... How could he eat such a concoction?

He stared down at his food, absorbed and transfixed at the delicious splendor sitting just a few inches from his face. He wanted to devour every last ounce of his delicious eggs... but at the same time... he wanted to flee.

For reasons unknown, Cody lifted his fork with a shaky hand, eyes fixated on the food but his mind ablaze with images of Carmen's hot cum coating the bowl. It was almost as if he was under some sort of trance. Like someone else was piloting his body and he was just a passenger. Because slowly his hand lowered and subsequently carved into the soft, yellow curdles, scooping up a forkful and bringing it back to his face. The smell of the rich eggs pervaded his nostrils. The flavor that he knew awaited called out to him, begging him to proceed and quell his hunger. Finally, after what seemed like hours, his body did what his mind dared contemplate, and brought the steamy, delicious food to his lips.

Sure enough it was ever so creamy and rich, probably thanks to Carmen's sticky secret. Nevertheless he swallowed, shuddering at how delicious it was. But then the realization hit him like a ton of bricks...

Her cum. He was eating Carmen's cum.

And despite every last hint of common sense signalled to him that he should be repulsed, this helping of scrambled eggs was the tastiest one yet. Semen or not, maybe it was all in his head. The thought of the secret ingredient that had gotten him hooked ever since he first ordered the café's scrambled eggs, and knowing that he was what was on Carmen's mind whenever she produced it... Somehow, awoke some foreign, tingling emotion within him.

Had he merely been flattered into liking it more, considering how rare it was for a girl to be attracted to him? Was it the erotic thrill of an employee doing something so kinky and forbidden? Perhaps there was simply a little masochist somewhere inside him that enjoyed being humiliated?

Or perhaps it was a combination of it all...

Strangely enough, the more Cody thought about it, the better the food seemed to taste, and the more excited he became. Every forkful he brought up to his mouth almost fell off, his entire arm shaking like crazy as he tried to contain the mix of emotions within him. Each time it reached his lips and the flavor hit his taste buds it was as if the strange and mysterious Carmen slowly etched herself into his mind, taking advantage of his carefree innocence. Each new bite made his blood burn hotter, like fire in his veins. *Was it her seed that was putting him under her spell? Spreading through his body and his heaving chest? Was it why he got so horny after breakfast?*

Before Cody knew it, the plate was empty. He didn't touch his bagel or his juice. He didn't even want it. Carmen's savory eggs had seemed to give him all the nutrients he needed. In just a few minutes he had completely devoured them, far faster than he ever had before, along with whatever traces of semen that came with them.

He took a deep breath, setting his fork down to stare at the barren plate. *What he had just done? And what she had done?* Carmen... the gorgeous, full-figured latina who always treated him with kindness and flattery, with a constant, beaming smile on her face. What was he to think of her now?

A jolt suddenly shook his body. The heat from the eggs that coursed through him sank to his nethers, and the tingling sensation rippled down to his groin and up his stiff boyhood. He gasped, feeling cum literally ooze out of his tip, half orgasm-half premature.

He looked down, noticing the ever-expanding stain of semen spreading across the front of his crotch. Suddenly, he had never been more turned on in his life. It *was* the eggs! It was the dickgirl semen that roused some sort of hidden lust. But how could he explain his soiled shorts if Carmen noticed?!

Eyes wide, Cody quickly rose from his seat, looking towards the reception to see if Carmen was there, but thankfully saw no trace of her. With a deep breath, he grabbed his backpack and bolted from his table on shaky legs. He kept an eye out for Carmen as he practically sprinted to the exit, knowing that if she were to see him now, she would no doubt get suspicious. Thankfully he remained unseen and out he ran into the still cold and dark surroundings of the early morning.

He couldn't stay in the café as he processed his feelings, that was for sure. Hell, he probably couldn't continue on with his school day as if nothing had happened either. His shorts were too tight. His erection was too much. And he absolutely had to change now that he had soiled himself.

Cody raced to his dorm. He didn't care if he was late for school. He needed release. He had to cum. So, as soon as he shut the door to his room he threw himself down on his bed, rolled over onto his back and yanked down the front of his shorts. His erect penis snapped out of his waistband, slapping him in the belly. It wasn't very big, but neither was he, and size didn't stop him from gripping the shaft tightly and stroking like a mad man.

A moan crossed his lips and he thrusted his hips off the mattress, holding his crotch in the air so he could watch himself work. He envisioned Carmen jacking off above him, stroking her mammoth cock that dwarfed his own. It didn't take long. And canted at his near-upside down angle, he opened his mouth and stuck out his tongue, firing a rope of cum at his own face. The first shot missed, splashing on his cheek, but the second and third hit his tongue. He lapped it up hungrily, hoping and yearning for it to taste as good as Carmen's.

He moaned again, relishing in his own flavor. It was satisfactory, but light years from Carmen's delectable seed...

A few seconds later and his dick shriveled and shrank, still dribbling semen like a wet, drooling pussy. Cody collapsed back on the bed, his mind still swimming with thoughts of his lusty, hispanic server.

Never before had such eroticism taken control of him like that. Not during puberty. Not during the hottest of porn. But with strangely newfound revelation, only when the taste of cum hit his lips...

Where the hell is he? Carmen thought to herself, resting her head in her hands. She checked her phone again. He was late. Tuesday morning, just like Monday, Cody was always there at six a.m. ready for breakfast. Now it was almost seven and other regulars had begun to arrive.

When the clock struck the hour a co-worker stepped from the backroom, greeting an anxious Carmen before heading off to take her first order.

Great, Carmen thought, *now I'll have to keep an eye out when I make Cody's eggs.*

She sighed, laying her arms down on the counter and planting her face in them. There was no doubt that she was being a bit silly about the whole thing. But this was the highlight of her day, damn it! The rest of her time spent at work was downright boring in comparison, not to mention stressful as of late. Her boss had promised more staff for quite some time, and yet the flyers in the windows with "We're Hiring" written in large letters remained.

The thought that Cody had suddenly fallen ill had crossed her mind. That would explain why he had acted so strange and flustered the day before, and why he left in such a hurry. What was even more frustrating was that she didn't get a chance to ask him out like she planned.

Her shorts swelled at the thought of him and she huffed another long sigh as she woefully came to terms that she may not see him today. *'Damnit!'* She huffed, *and she had such a load for him too!* And she had purposefully not jerked off all day yesterday to make sure he received the plentiful serving he deserved this morning!

Then, the sound she was hoping for finally came. The bell above the entrance door rang, and off the counter she rose, suddenly on full alert as she looked up to see who had entered. It was Cody! Carmen couldn't contain her excitement.

"Wel-" she began before the sight of the boy stopped her greeting.

Holy-fucking-shit what was he wearing!?

His typical smile was nowhere to be found, and in its place was a nervous, flushed look of indifference and lucidity. While still skin tight and more fit for a thin girl rather than a boy, Cody's current shirt was devoid of any modesty. He was wearing a white crop top with pink lettering on the front where breasts would normally be there to accentuate them. The hem didn't reach all the way down to his tight, flat tummy either, showing off a hint of skin between the top and his shorts. His cute little belly button would occasionally peek out as he walked. Though strutted may have been the better word…

Carmen scanned him as stealthily as she could, noticing that his waistline wasn't the only thing that was exposed. His shirt wasn't merely a crop top, it was an off-the-shoulder one as well, showing off his smooth, slender form from the top of his arm to his collarbones. As he approached she could read the writing on his shirt's front - SLUT.

Carmen swallowed hard, stunned as the lithe, beautiful little creature sauntered over to the counter. She could hardly believe what she was seeing. It was her dear Cody no doubt, but by any other accounts he looked like a full-fledged girl!

His shorts too were equally sexy. Small and tight like normal, they left little to the imagination. The boy's thick thighs stuck out from the tiny garments as if they were two sizes too small, and one could easily see the small purse of boy parts nestled in a small, plump pouch in their front. Carmen relished in what the backside would look like, salivating at the tiny bit of fabric nearly invisible wedged between his two, hefty ass cheeks.

Not only were his clothes radically feminine but his hair too, now trimmed in a 'bob-like' style just above his shoulders. Carmen watched wide-eyed as Cody brushed back a lock of his blond hair behind his ear as he made his way towards her with nervous steps. Completely forgetting about her sense of professionalism, she stared at his revealed waistline, immediately conjuring up fantasies of covering his flat little tummy and cute belly button in a thick layer of cum…

God, was he teasing her? Carmen wondered.

"Umm…" Cody reached the counter and looked back at the awe-struck latin amazon. "H-hey Carmen…"

Snapping out of it upon hearing his adorable, androgynous voice, Carmen only then realized that he was standing right in front of her. "O-oh, yeah! Hey, sorry!" she stammered. "Cody uh, wow. Would you like… the usual?"

Containing herself with the now crossdressed boy had never been this hard. Oh, to just reach out and snatch him up, then pull him over the counter and onto his knees…

"Yes…" Cody said quietly, batting his eyes.

Carmen cleared her throat, trying her best not to let Cody's tight little body distract her any further. "A-alright! I'll get on it right away!" She looked at him, hoping that her bubbly mood would prove contagious, but all he did was silently look down into his wallet as he dug for money. He glanced at her a final time, then put down the exact amount needed to pay for his standard meal, before spinning around and leaving for his usual seat in the corner of the café.

As much as Carmen loved the view of his thick, bubble butt, Cody's new clothes and strange mannerisms left her confused more than anything. But hey, she wasn't about to look a gift horse in the mouth or disappoint him by delaying his breakfast. With another glance at his plump rear end, she headed into the breakroom, hoping to quickly empty her balls, using Cody's new outfit as inspiration. It was going to be tough to last long with his sinful look fresh in her brain.

Carmen was practically bursting out of her shorts when she slammed the break room door behind her, scooping up the mixing bowl she kept nearby. There was no one else there and she just couldn't contain herself. In a flash she tossed the bowl on the far table and yanked open her fly, snapping off the button and sending it hurdling into the wall.

"Shit," Carmen huffed, thinking only briefly of how to explain the missing button. But the folds of her shorts unfurled, and her fat, swollen cock pulled her zipper down on its own, exposing her hot flesh to the cool air of the room. She gasped, looking down as her womanhood lurched out of its prison like an anaconda uncoiling. Free from restraint it hardened instantly, soon sticking out at a near perfect ninety degree angle. It was time. She let her imagination flow free. The images in her head of Cody in his new, sexy outfit quickly morphed into an erotic ensemble as she reached down with her strong right hand and gripped her cock mid-shaft.

She bit her lip, shivering as she took the first few strokes. Pre-cum was already leaking. Her eyes rolled over white, and she began to work her fleshy pole.

In Carmen's mind, Cody had assumed many different roles, ranging from things as low as a street whore, to schoolgirl, naughty maid, to her very own spouse, all to fit whatever mood she was in at the time. This time he was a stripper, wearing the exact thing he had on just now. But now he was a dancer slowly and seductively sauntering towards her in a dark room, his hungry eyes locked onto hers and his adorable face burning with lust. His fingers were pulling away at the bottom of his top, revealing more and more of his creamy skin, while his unbuttoned shorts slowly slid down his girly thighs in an equally slow manner. Carmen had regrettably never gotten as much as a glimpse of his underwear in real life, but that didn't stop her from imagining a thin white thong hugging his voluptuous butt and cute little package in the front, all now slowly being revealed in front of her. At the same time came those small, pink buds for nipples that his shirt got stuck on as he pulled on it in an oh so drawn-out and teasing fashion.

"Um… Hey…" a meek, androgynous voice chimed from behind her.

Just like that, bliss turned to horror. Carmen may have been near lost in her fantasy, but she knew that she *hadn't* imagined Cody's voice. A chill that reached into her very core suddenly froze her in place and the vigorous stroking of her cock came to a swift, immediate halt.

Straightening her back, Carmen turned her head towards the door behind her, knowing inevitably, who she would see. Cody, in his white crop top hanging off one shoulder, the words 'Slut' emblazoned on its chest, his tiny short shorts wrapped around his voluptuous thighs, stood there staring back at her. Carmen felt the judgment in those eyes, the way anyone might glare when they catch someone masturbating…

"C-Cody?!" she blurted, "You… you can't be in here!" Her words did nothing to ease the tension. There was no way for her to deny what she was doing. She had been caught in the act. But instead of bursting into anger or overt surprise, Cody lingered in place, silent and coy.

Carmen stammered out a curse in Spanish, then painfully tucked her rock-hard cock back inside her tiny shorts. She turned, trying to cram more of her meat into hiding, finding that Cody's judgmental gaze was immediately drawn to the fat bulge in her front. She managed to get most of it jammed inside but the zipper would not stay up and there was no button to sinch them closed. Looking down, she realized there was still quite a bit for the boy to see - the shaft of her cock coiled up out of the opening. What could possibly have been going on inside his head at that moment was impossible to tell, but just as she had convinced herself that her life was over, the look on his face seemed to change ever so slightly. Perhaps Carmen was imagining it, but in moving his eyes from her face to her bulge, the look on Cody's face seemed to soften.

"Wait..." he said, his stiff legs stepping into the room.

"... Huh?" Carmen replied, trying to cover her shame with both hands. But Cody stepped towards her, holding out a hand as if to stop her. "W-what are you doing?!"

The spastic movement of her fumbling fingers trying to close her fly was abruptly halted, by none other than Cody's own tiny, delicate hand. Already having made his way up to Carmen, he placed digits atop hers, signalling to keep her fly open. She looked down at it in disbelief, before looking up at his face, by then mere inches away from her own.

She had never seen him this closely before, let alone in such a state. The way he stared at her with those big, beautiful eyes that twinkled a vibrant blue color, the way his sweet breath flowed past those perfect, pink lips of his. Indeed, the look of accusation from a moment ago had been replaced entirely by what seemed like... longing.

Suddenly Carmen's hand on her crotch was firmly but affectionately clutched by Cody's, while his other hand reached around her waist. He pulled the two of them together, his flat chest mashing against her pert B-Cups and stiff nipples. Being noticeably shorter than Carmen he raised up on his toes and leaned in for a bold kiss. When their lips touched he laid into her, thighs, waists, chests and stomach all squished against each other as the pair shared their first ever moment of affection.

Carmen, whose mouth still hung open in shock, had no chance of reacting to Cody's tongue slipping past her lips. Before she knew it he was already making out with her, at first without any sort of reciprocation. But it didn't take long for her to relax just enough to close her eyes and return the surprise, sudden kiss.

While Carmen had until now thought of Cody as shy and timid, she hadn't expected the vigor and expertise with which he kissed her. He made sure to hold them tightly together with his arm, fondling the front of her shorts, while at the same time keeping her in place with his lips as his tongue coiled within her mouth. Carmen at last began kissing him back, their lips smacking against each other and their chins glistening from their mixed saliva.

So intense was their intimate moment that Carmen barely registered that Cody suddenly pulled away from her, lowering his heels to the floor. The tall latina opened her groggy eyes to see the earlier hint of longing in the face of her crush enhanced tenfold. He stared at her with a bite of his lip, still holding on to her with an arm around her midsection and a hand against her own that had yet to let go of her zipper. From there he went on to gently pry it away from her fly, with Carmen in a daze that rendered her unable to even think about stopping him. With her hand out of the way, the next thing she felt was Cody's fingers rubbing against her coiled yet stiff cock, coaxing a moan from her wet lips.

"Wha... Cody? What are you doing?" Carmen was finally able to mutter.

Cody leaned in again, getting his lips as close to Carmen's ear as he could. "I want it straight from the source this time..." he whispered.

His feminine, tender voice reverberated in her mouth. She nearly came right then and there. But then his fingertips found the hem of her shorts and slithered underneath, touching more of her flesh. Her knees started buckling, and had it not been for the table behind her that she had been holding onto, she would no doubt have collapsed.

"You... you want to..." she began, seeing Cody's lust-drunk eyes. "How did you know...?"

"I saw you," he said. At that point his hand was rubbing against Carmen's fat bulge, almost jerking her off from outside her shorts. "I saw what you did to my food..."

Carmen gulped in embarrassment, but her horny mind simultaneously started to take over. "I'm sorry... I just thought it would be hot..."

Blushing and nervous as he may have been, Cody nonetheless smirked at her. "Oh, it was," he said, the hand he had around Carmen's midsection sliding back to her front, joining in on teasingly caressing her cock. "Gross, humiliating, unprofessional... but also hot. And sooo fucking delicious..."

With his petrifying gaze still fixed on Carmen's glistening, brown eyes, he hooked his thumbs underneath her shorts and gently began tugging on them. Even as they slowly unveiled the massive thing hidden underneath, Cody knew not to give in to his curiosity immediately, and thus refrained from looking down to see it in the flesh. He didn't know what he would feel upon witnessing it up close for the first time, but he knew that his reaction would give away some degree of shock, fear and perhaps even submission.

"Wait..." Carmen pleaded, her cock fully exposed as the hem of her shorts continued down around her full, bronze balls. "We can't... Not here..."

"Oh, I'm sorry, is this room for masturbation only?" Cody retorted snappily. Letting go of her legwear that were now lodged mid-thigh, under a low-hanging nutsack, he knelt, grabbed her dick by the base and gave it a long, slow stroke all the way to the spongy tip. "Or are blowjobs not allowed??"

Carmen gulped, feeling her cock twitch. "W-what if someone sees us?"

"Then we better be quick about it..." Cody said, kneeling before leaning in and kissing the top of her shaft. His lips sent a shudder through her body and the boy's knees folded together to hit the floor at last.

With his head at perfect viewing level, Cody nearly went cross-eyed at what his hands had already been introduced to. He was still holding it, squeezing it, feeling its warmth, but his mind was immediately overwhelmed by the sight and, to some extent, smell of girlcock. It throbbed inches from his face, a puddle of precum already having formed on the floor beneath, and continuing to grow from the absurd dripping.

A heavy gasp escaped his mouth, and with it, his demeanor changed in the exact way he had expected. To think that one glimpse of the beautiful phallus the day before was all it took for him to fantasize about getting to see it again... Well, perhaps those thoughts mostly revolved around the creamy reward it inevitably would grant him, but still... Her thick, circumcised cock was nothing short of a beauty in his eyes. The sheer length, almost ten inches, the girth, which his fingers weren't even close to reaching around, the beautiful, caramel skin that covered it, lined with thick veins that throbbed in tandem with the rest of the shaft... How could he resist it? And considering his general disinterest in sex, how could anyone?

Using his other hand to complete his grip on the thing, Cody's suppressed desires could be held back no more. He closed his eyes and leaned forward, perching the sticky slit against his cute, up-turned nose, smearing the entrance of his nostrils and upper lip with precum. Not a second was wasted in taking in the scent of Carmen's gorgeous cock, and to his delight, it was equally as erotic as the way it looked and felt. It was but a mild smell of both natural musk and a hint of fruity, vanilla body wash, but the effect that it had on Cody was all the stronger.

Even the tiny amount of precum that seeped into his mouth was nothing short of delicious, enhancing his lust even further. Pressing one palm against the side of the shaft, his lips continued down the opposite side, dragging across the veiny skin until he came all the way down to the base. Without pause, hesitation, or even a hint of shame, he deftly slid down Carmen's ballsack, immediately sucking one of her big sperm tanks into his mouth.

"Ah..." Carmen moaned, looking down at Cody as he leaned his head back with her testicle between his pouting lips, pulling the skin of her hairless scrotum taut. He held it there a moment, looking up at her with a baseball-sized testicle between his lips, suckling on it the way one might wittle on a piece of candy. Then Cody let her nut fall out of his mouth with a wet plop, sending them both swinging back and forth like a wet pendulum. They quickly came to a still in his left hand while his right squeezed the shaft, and his mouth came diving down to instantly wrap around Carmen's thick, ever-leaking cockhead.

"Oh my god..." the quivering latina blurted. Virtually every square inch of her genitals being stimulated: Her pulsating shaft by a hand squeezing and pulling on it as if milking it; her glans by a beautiful pair of pink boy-lips; and her balls by a gentle massage of Cody's fingers.

The femboy's mouth was far better than anything she had imagined so many times. Cody, whose eyes had been all too focused on the massive, brown cock he was worshipping, looked up at the gorgeous girl it was attached to. She was in ecstasy, tilting her head back and cupping a breast with her left hand, still holding herself up with the right. So far he had only treated his blowjob as something to please himself with, his own curiosity being the motivation. But seeing that he seemed to already have caused her untold pleasure despite his lack of experience sent a shiver of excitement through his girly little body.

"Mmm, that's so good you nasty little slut." Carmen purred.

Sliding his lips back off Carmen's cock, Cody momentarily ceased his worshipping, his hand grasping it firmly at the base. "Am I living up to your expectations?" he said teasingly, showing off his perfectly white teeth in a slutty grin.

"F-fuck yes..." She purred.

"You wanna feed me like this from now on?" he purred, slowly licking the rim of her glans before popping the cockhead back in his mouth.

"Every fucking day, *puta*..." Carmen said, putting an instinctive latin emphasis on the word.

Cody giggled with the juicy cockhead in his mouth and his hand began moving back and forth across the veiny shaft once more. "I'm a hungry boy, though..." he said, removing it only briefly to quickly huff out his words. "You think you can keep me full?"

"Mmhmm!" Carmen replied without pause, biting her lip and pinching a nipple.

"Well then," Cody gobbled between his words, "I think it's feeding time..."

Lolling out his dripping tongue, Cody leaned in to pick up where he left off. The hard cock was plunged several inches deep into his mouth without hesitation, and his lips immediately clung to its surface like he was some slutty bimbo trying to wring it out.

"Ooh, shit..." Carmen moaned. Her jaw slowly went slack, stretching the thick, red-painted lips of her wide mouth open fully, a dribble of drool running down her chin. She could barely even see at this point, stars beginning to bespeckle her vision as her long, dark eyelashes fluttered out of control.

And though it wasn't really visible, Cody was in a similar boat. It was as if the flow of heat from Carmen's thick precum was feeding the ravenous butterflies in his stomach and the beating of his heart. Even so, the blush on his cheeks wasn't merely induced by lust, but also embarrassment. He couldn't believe the words that he had just uttered, nor the way he had just waltzed into the breakroom to almost immediately drop down to his knees and offer a blowjob like it was nothing.

There was but one explanation... He was meant for this. At the very core of his being was a slutty little femboy who was born to suck big, fat, throbbing girl-cocks. He had never come across a girl like Carmen before, so perhaps it wasn't all that strange that his sexuality had remained largely unexplored in the past... But now it was all clear to him. The spark of lust caused from just one quick glance and a few fleeting tastes had ignited into a full-blown inferno of desire, worship and depravity as he continued to give the sloppiest head he was capable of.

Determined to bring Carmen to orgasm, Cody went a step further. His hands let go of the shaft and nutsack entirely, instead taking a moment to relax and breath through his nose. He placed his palms on Carmen's smooth, toned thighs and found a new angle for his throat. Craning his neck and aligning his esophagus, he hunched forward, opening his jaw. With that, the resulting few inches that he was forced to slide forward introduced his completely inexperienced throat to the huge womanhood occupying his mouth. While not as deep as to enter it, he pressed the glans firmly against the entrance of his throat, feeling it rub against his tonsils to the point where it almost forced itself past them.

"Oh my god! Such a good boy!" Carmen exclaimed. Now, with more than half of her cock buried within Cody's mouth, her body could no longer keep up. Her legs started spasming from the overbearing pleasure of the pair of lips squeezing her shaft, while a nimble little tongue tickled its underside, and the room soon became a blurry mess before her eyes. She was close, and yet she knew she had to do something to speed things up further, since the fear of getting caught still lingered.

Almost as if she had read Cody's mind, the one thing he had hoped for happened. He felt Carmen put her palm against the top of his head, to then softly and slowly give his hair a stroke down along its backside. From there she bunched up his gorgeous, shoulder-length locks into a tuft and held onto it with a grip so strong that a boy like Cody could never escape it.

The intense slurping and sucking noises only got louder as a result, as did the speed at which Cody bobbed his head with the thick cock pressing against the back of his throat. He was gagging to some extent, but he didn't care. He couldn't help himself. There was just something so hot about being held in place like a good little cocksucker while his own mind likewise was set on not stopping until the climax was reached. As if both his inner slut and Carmen were working together to teach him the standard of what every blowjob should be like. His own penis was just an afterthought at that point: A tiny little thing that twitched eagerly within his shorts while a superior cock was getting all the attention.

With teary eyes and the entrance to his throat being battered from the way Carmen plunged her cock against it, Cody looked up at her as if begging for her cum. Partly due to exhaustion, but more so because the intense craving that had been building up since the day before was about to drive him crazy.

Carmen's cock only throbbed and ached harder as a result of the beautiful view, and her rather suppressed moans were starting to force their way out of her mouth at a volume that could potentially be heard by customers and staff. Of course, it was far beyond her power to stop herself. She had anticipated caution and grace from Cody's pretty, pink lips, but instead they were damn near sucking the soul out of her. Even if she had wanted to stop for whatever reason, it would have been impossible to tear him off.

As Cody both felt and saw Carmen's body start to shudder and slump together, he at last went in for what neither he nor she were prepared for. One final, deep breath filled his lungs as he pulled back, and with that, he managed to use the last of his fortitude to relax his every muscle. The fat, slick cock slid in along his lips and tongue once more, but its soft tip now easily found its way further than ever. Cody's teary eyes rolled back from the suffocating, yet strangely tingling feeling of having his throat stretched open. Her hot, throbbing balls on his face assured it, he had taken it all.

Carmen looked down, cupping the boy's pretty face in her hands. His eyes were white, rolled into the back of his skull. Tears and eyeliner streaked down his face. His lips and nose were literally covered in pre-cum and saliva. He had the entire length of her mammoth cock submerged. It was a thing of beauty.

And so, the breaking point was reached for the sweaty, gorgeous latina. Her sperm-churning balls that rested against Cody's drool-covered neck were practically boiling on the inside, and thus they signaled to the rest of her body that it was time. With newfound energy, she gritted her teeth and squeezed the boy's neck in an attempt to extract as much scalding cum as possible. In that moment, they both silently decided that neither of them were leaving until Carmen's cock had been thoroughly milked.

"Oh fuck! Cody..." she gasped. "I'm gonna cummm..."

Remaining locked in place, Cody could feel the underside of Carmen's thick cock swell up as a load of cum barrelled through it. Like a liquid freight train thundering through a biological tunnel. Cody thought he was ready for what was coming, but his lust and bliss were replaced by pure shock as the back of his throat was suddenly covered in the hot, creamy substance. Even after the first shot subsided, the throbbing shaft down his throat inflated with surges of cum over and over, filling up his gullet quicker than it could empty into his hungry stomach. Part of him wanted to abandon what he had started, but his goal had already been set in stone. Despite his struggle for air and the gurgling pressure of cum building up in his throat, it was just way too hot to put an end to such a memorable moment already.

Carmen, struggling to even stand up, gripped the boy's head, lurched forward and thrust her pelvis in one final, violent maneuver. Then simultaneously let out a sharp, hissing scream from brain-melting pleasure. "FFFFUUUUCK!" she growled. "Swallow it whore. Drink my cum you slutty, *puta* bitch!"

Cody did just that. But while it seemed that the vice-like pressure of Cody's mouth was far from weakening, Carmen couldn't take it anymore. With each of her limbs quivering, she finally let go of the pretty little bundle of hair in her hand, then leaned back against the counter behind her once more with a satisfied smile on her face, her muscles still rhythmically contracting with each burst of semen.

Finally released from her grip, Cody slowly pulled back, letting the veiny appendage slide up and out, eventually enough to free the fat cockhead that was plugged into it and allowing him a big gasp of fresh air, but kept the cum-leaking tip in his mouth. After all, it was the flavor he was after. He sat there on his knees, panting like a dog while staring up at Carmen's beautiful face through his teary, shameful eyes, all while her final, comparatively weak ejections of cum poured out across his taste buds.

At last Carmen was spent, and to say that she was impressed with Cody was to put it lightly. "You..." she huffed, looking down at the pretty boy as he popped her brown cock out from between his pink lips. "You took it all..."

If possible, Cody would have flashed her a victorious grin, but his mouth was occupied with something more important. In order to savor the sweet, yet savory flavor of Carmen's thick cum, he had made sure to let it fill up his entire oral cavity, and held off on swallowing for the moment. His cheeks bulged out like balloons, containing a volume so large that a trickle of white had forced its way out between his puckered lips and down his chin.

"God, that's so fucking hot..." said Carmen. She couldn't believe what had become of the calm, sweet boy that she thought she knew, but she loved it nevertheless. More than anything, she was just happy. Happy that something as shameful as cumming in a customer's food could lead to something like this. As far as she knew, Cody was the perfect match for her. Even putting aside his kindness, gorgeous face and supple body, he seemed to have a horny, kinky side to match it. Perhaps he could be even more kinky...

"Show me." Carmen commanded.

Cody immediately complied, parting his lips and showing the gathered pool of girlcum beyond them. Additionally, he stuck out his tongue and swirled it around, sending ripples throughout the sticky, viscous liquid. It clearly went appreciated by Carmen, judging not only from how the longing look on her face made her seem ready to pounce on Cody, but also from the sudden twitch in her softening cock that hung before his face.

Finally he swallowed the fat load, before licking his smirking lips. "Thanks for the meal... It was delicious."

"Another happy customer," Carmen replied playfully.

"I'll be ordering the same thing from now on," Cody said, standing up and using his index finger to gather up the line of cum on his chin. He proceeded to bring it to his mouth, sucking it down with his pouting lips while seductively staring into Carmen's brown eyes. "Consider this my new 'usual'."

The pair smiled at one another. But suddenly, footsteps could be heard coming from the adjacent room. "Shit! Someone's coming!" Carmen blurted, immediately beginning to fumble with putting her sticky, hanging cock back in her shorts. She managed to zip her fly up past her half-chub, but there was still no button, so she tugged her already tight shirt down hard to cover her midriff.

Cody scrambled to his feet while fixing his hair. Carmen had really done a number on him, but he quickly got it back to the way it gently flowed down his head and neck.

The door opened, and a middle-aged man stepped inside. It was Sam Roberts, the owner of Café Sirénes and he noticed the pair, red faced and awkward. He shot Carmen a quizzical look before looking over to the crossdressed young boy.

"Ah, Cody!" he beamed, looking pleasantly surprised. "You're already here!"

Mr. Roberts came closer, waving, seemingly recognizing him.

"Y-yep," Cody mumbled in response. "Carmen here showed me around a bit..."

Mr. Roberts turned to the tall, latin amazon, her hands still clamped down over her crotch. His look changed from curious to affirmation. "Good initiative, Carmen. I can always count on you."

"... Huh?" Carmen mumbled, utterly confused.

What was going on here? She wondered. *Why were they talking as if they knew each other?*

"Well then, Cody," said Mr. Roberts, seemingly in too giddy a state to even notice Carmen's confusion. "I'll go get some things from my office, then I'll teach you all you need to know. You ladies finish up here in the meantime, okay?"

"S-sure, Mr. Roberts." Cody sheepishly smiled back. "I can't wait." It felt embarrassing to stand there, talking to the owner of the café in his girly, white shirt that showed off his shoulders and midriff, but it had been worth it just to make his first time with Carmen a little bit more special.

Mr. Roberts turned on his heels and left just as quickly as he had entered.

"Um... Cody? What the hell is going on? What was he talking about?" Carmen blurted.

"Well," the cute boy began with a little blush. "I applied for the waitress job. Aaand he... might think I'm a girl." He giggled, still totally passable in his sexy little outfit. "Aaand today's my first day. Surprise!"

"W-what?!" Carmen exclaimed in a bright smile. "You little slut. Is that the only reason you wore that today?!"

Cody blew her a kiss, winked, then headed for the door, turning just as his hand gripped the knob.

JORDAN BAILEY

"Well, not only..."

THE END

THE END

STRANDED

My tragically poor choices led me aboard a luxury cruise line in the desperate attempt to find a partner. Perhaps a handsome young man with an open mind, or even a rich, older gentleman who saw my body as some sort of bucket list kink. However, neither of these came to pass, and none of the possibilities I had hoped for came to fruition. Because now I was in a broken down life raft, drifting in the heat and stillness of South Pacific waters.

Luck was never my strong suit. Not with my relationships, or lack thereof, not my sexuality, being an almost thirty year transwoman, and certainly not in my current predicament. No, it was my business sense and smarts that gifted me a life of wealth and high fashion, but like a double edged sword, it also landed me in my current predicament.

So here it was that I, Maxine Christiensen, an entrepreneur with the money and time to indulge the whim of sailing the world, was now thirsty and sunburnt, slowly dying on the open sea. It had been almost a week, at least I think so. Water ran out two days ago, and the only food I had, sank with the boat. There were no other survivors either, at least none that came to the surface with me that night.

I tried to cover myself as much as possible, as my pale, icelandic skin was no match for the elements. My hair too, if I wasn't already a stark, almost-platinum blonde, would have been bleached by the sun by now.

So delirious was I that when I spotted a tiny speck on the horizon, I almost didn't take notice. Maybe it was dehydration, or I just believed my mind was playing tricks, that I didn't flinch until I got closer. Sure enough the current pulled my raft close, slowly increasing the object's size as I closed in. The speck soon turned into a quaint little island, complete with palm trees, a lagoon and a crystal white beach.

When I crawled to the nearest rim of my barely floating raft, soaking in the sight of that island, I think my blue eyes sparkled more than the ocean itself. Where there was land there must be life, and with any luck, civilization! Any that could put me back in touch with the modern world. No doubt my family and business had been notified of the crash, and thus they would be searching for me. I was afterall the only 'daughter' and a wealthy aire to the Christiensen name.

As soon as my makeshift boat came within reach of the lagoon I clamored to shore. Stepping on the wet sand I fell to my knees, gripping land at last. I rested for a few minutes, almost breaking into tears, then made my way up to the tree line, deciding to follow it around.

I thought about the view of the island I'd seen from the ocean. Though I hadn't seen any signs of structures or docks, surely if there was something it would be visible from my path.

Whilst exploring my new realm, I knew one of my first tasks would be to find fresh water. And not but a few yards from where I landed, I noticed a path into the brush, which raised my hopes considerably. A worn track testified to animals, or even humans, wearing it down through constant use. It was a good sign to be sure. Deciding to follow it, I had to crouch and push aside overarching branches. Whatever made or frequented the trail must have been no taller than four or five feet.

After following the path for only a few yards, it opened up into a vision of paradise: a large open clearing of tropical trees surrounding a crystal clear pool of water, fed by a small yet beautiful waterfall. I sauntered in with a smile, awestruck at the oasis's beauty. I felt like a fairy tale princess amidst a garden grove.

Once I reached the pond, I fell to my knees and hurriedly cupped handfuls of the water. I knew it was fresh, not just from its taste but because it fed from somewhere deeper on the island.

Immediately my body felt rejuvenated. It tasted so good! I drank and drank, careful not to overload my parched organs. When I had my fill I splashed the liquid on my face, quite literally feeling it heal my damaged skin. Afterwards I did my best to clean myself, mostly tending to my burnt shoulders and thighs, my once perfect complexion torn asunder. I pouted, running my hands over my poor limbs, but at least I was alive...

I considered diving into the water. Letting the hydration soothe my sunburnt facade, but thought better of it in case this lagoon was my only source of freshwater. Instead, after another gulp, I found the shade of a palm tree home and laid down amongst the fallen leaves. Without the boiling scope of the sun I felt finally at ease, and closed my eyes...

I must have dozed off. Because the next thing I knew, I heard voices! Two or more people conversing animatedly, and in English! I shook myself but couldn't move. There were more voices, young sounding, like children, and they were whispering and tittering amongst themselves.

A dream, I said to myself. I was dreaming. Listfully swooning over chipper voices.

Until I realized that I wasn't!

I wanted to jump up and run to the sounds. Sprint and holler and hug whoever was out there. But I quickly thought the better of it being on a strange, foreign island. Instead I shifted to my hands and knees, and quietly made my way towards the mysterious voices.

Crawling closer, I peered around the bush and saw two young boys, teenagers at most. They were wearing what looked like the remnants of shorts, and nothing else, which barely covered anything. In fact, their makeshift 'loin cloths' really just barely covered their genitals, because their fleshy backsides were exposed, with cloth so scant that both bubbly, tanned, butts were almost on full display.

They stood knee deep in the water practically naked, their bodies bronze and lithe. I was surprised, but not exactly shocked. For years I thought I was a lesbian, but now, looking at their obtuse, round and quite feminine backsides, I found myself intrigued. I could not help noticing how undeveloped they were, with no no hair on their chests or under their armpits. I noticed too that, each wore curves more akin to a woman, with wide hips and thick thighs, much like my own.

They were both blonde, one's hair darker than the other, but not naturally. It appeared they were both a light shade of brunette at some point, but had been out in the sun for too long, giving them both, golden chestnut hues. down to their shoulders and appearing crudely cut. I was surprised at the affection that I was already feeling toward these two strangers, and the interest their bodies had for me. I put it down to my thankfulness at finding some sign of humanity and civilization, as well as to the natural beauty of the boy's coltish figures.

I watched them for God knows how long, frolicking and laughing, splashing water on one another. As they played, their shorts soaked, and I could make out the outlines of small erections within.

My own blood pumped. I could feel it move like sludge in my veins, all leading to my most vital organ. I licked my lips watching them, never before so enthralled in men until now.

I must have slipped or nudged a rock, or perhaps my breathing had become too heavy, because suddenly the darker haired boy squeaked and grabbed his partner.

"Oh my god," one of the boys said, pointing at my exact location.

I realize now I probably wasn't hiding well. Nor could I. I had just been behind some low stones and short grass, not nearly enough to hide my hulking form.

"It's okay!" I shouted, standing quickly, holding out my palms.

I'm not sure who was more frightened, them or me.

"She's so pretty," the shorter, lighter haired boy said under his breath. It was no more than a whisper, no doubt meant to only be heard by his friend.

"Who… who are you?" The taller boy said.

What a sight I must have been. At six-foot-four I was no little girl, and my long blonde but disheveled hair was frayed and dehydrated, barely held together by my thick nordic braid over one shoulder. My makeup was history, taken by the ocean's waves, but my eyes remained an icy blue.

"My name's Max. Er, Maxine. I was on a boat. It crashed and… I washed ashore here."

"A boat?" The first boy said. "Does it work? Does it float?"

"Um, no… The boat sank. I escaped on a life raft, and it just happened to bring me here."

They both sulked, the brief glimmer of hope in their eyes vanishing. I was thankful for the lull. In fact, I was having trouble concentrating on responding to his question, mesmerized by my companions' beauty.

"W-wait, what are you doing here? Are you alone?" The words clumsily spilled out of my mouth. "Where did you come from?"

The shorter boy spoke up, still clutching the other boys' arm. "We were marooned here when our plane crashed about a year ago. Our headmaster…

"Teacher." The taller boy interjected.

"Yes. Our teacher, Misses Williams. And the pilot. They… they died. There' six of us now. Six of us left…"

"Six… of you boys?" I asked, crestfallen.

They both nodded. The little one finished, "Mmmhmm. It's just us."

'Plane crash?' I pondered, looking them over. I don't remember any plane crashes of note. I even tried to keep tabs on such things to format any highs or lows in stocks, trends or shifts in the numerous markets I had my fingers in.

As though reading my thoughts, the taller boy responded. "Chartered flight from England. We're from a private school. Something happened with the engine, I think. Our pilot saw the island and took us down into the water nearby. Said we were lucky to find any kind of land before he...."

"He didn't make it?" I said. More statement than question.

Both the boys shook their heads.

My heart sank. "And no radio? Phone? Anything?"

Their looks answered my questions.

"How have you survived?" I asked.

"We make do. We were scouts back home," the tall one said. I couldn't help but notice how his friend held on to him during the entire back and forth, as though I were speaking to a man and wife, they clung together.

As this odd conversation continued, my gaze returned back to the fact that these two boys, quite handsome, beautiful really, were still nearly naked and for whatever reason hadn't felt the need to dress. Their slim, tan bodies caused a feeling in me that I had trouble classifying at first.

My mind racked. It was so hot. Blood seemed to have pooled in my lower half and stayed there. Standing up once more I felt light headed.

`My name's Mickey, by the way," the taller, darker haired boy said. "And this is Kris," he smiled at his companion and they unashamedly kissed in front of me.

"Kris with a K," Kris said with a smile.

I nodded. At least I think I did, but as I did my world spun. A stark blackness followed, and I saw myself somehow, like a spirit rising out of my body, crumple to the forest floor.

The next thing I knew I was staring up into the sky, a thin veil of cloth over my eyes. I realized I was moving, levitating off the forest floor. I tried to turn my head but everything was blurry. I still felt lightheaded and dizzy. I pulled the cloth off my face and tried to scan my surroundings, but it was all a haze. Yet as my vision began to clear I could see the figures around me. They were carrying me!

"Shh. You were out in the sun too long. Rest now," I heard Mickey say, putting a cool rag on my forehead. "We're taking you back to the group. Try and relax."

We traveled for what felt like an eternity. It was hard to gauge because I kept slipping in and out of consciousness. But as the sun began to set, I found myself in a makeshift encampment they'd apparently created in an area engulfed by palm trees. It was a clearing some thirty or forty feet around, with a campfire in the center surrounded by small tents.

They carried me into the largest tent where I was once more garnished with shade. Once they sat me down I felt a canteen at my lips, then cool water.

Finally I sat up, noticing the makeshift stretcher I was on. There was some sort of lotion or ointment on my shoulders and arms. It smelled of coconut. Had the boys applied it while I was asleep? If so, they may be more brash than one might assume, touching an older woman in such a vulnerable state. I wasn't complaining mind you, because now instead of smelling of sea salt and sweat, a lush, tropical fragrance filled my nostrils.

Outside, I could hear more voices whispering to one another. Occasionally I would catch someone or peeking into my tent, then watch them skitter away like a mouse.

Mickey the tall, darker haired boy appeared, clutching a bowl of leafy greens, like some Gilligan's Island salad.

"Here you go, Missus Maxine. It isn't much. But it's something." He said as he offered it to me.

I took it happily and smiled, quickly plucking a crisp, cool bit of lettuce into my mouth.

"You're safe here. We've made it this far. We'll protect you too, Miss Maxine."

"Max is fine, dear. Really." I smiled, trying to pry my eyes off his trim, coltish legs. "But who's outside? How many of you are here?"

Mickey smiled, stuck two fingers in his mouth, and whistled loudly. There was a scamper of tiny foot falls outside, like a herd of puppies scrambling for food. The sharp cry summoned a rabble from outside, and in the next instant, six lean, half-naked boys were in my tent.

Four more boys, all young like Mickey and Kris, joined the pair. They were each cute, athletic, and slightly effeminate, with cherubique faces, plushy backsides and big, sparkling eyes. Kris introduced them with a wave of his hand, "This is Andi, Mattie, Harley and Ricky," he said, presenting each as he spoke their names. Guys? This is Miss Maxine."
--List and describe them all? Reduce number?
Blonde, Brunette, Redhead, short hair, long hair

They all let out a shy but collective, "HI!" as if they were in a school play.

I blushed, nodded and waved. "Just Max. Please."

The boys were all about what you'd expect, perhaps a bit skinnier from their year-long ordeal. Hair fair and scraggly, at various lengths, gangly limbs, deep tans over their lithe, hairless bodies. Like Mickey and Kris, the other four were scantily clad as well, merely dressed in rags or loincloths fashioned from animal hide.

"My, my," I said, looking over each of their tender, curvy figures. "I'm impressed that you all are still alive and doing so well after an entire year alone."

Mikey nodded, "It's because we stick together. We care about each other. We had to!"

"I can see that," I giggled.

After a short while they visibly relaxed and invited me to stay, and I accepted. As it turned out, their flight had been well packed with supplies, though not nearly enough to sustain six boys for a year. They had used their recently acquired foraging skills to secure protein and the few edible root crops on the island.

After dinner they showed me the sleeping arrangements, three beds constructed with branches and leaves, and supplies from the plane to serve as shelter covers and blankets. I said that I probably had something on the boat that I could jerry rig as a bed for myself.

They laughed. "Oh, no Miss, we would be honored if you would take the biggest tent. You are the oldest afterall. We were always told to treat a woman with the utmost respect. Besides, we are so very glad you're here!"

My look of confusion brought them to giggling. "We've been waiting for your arrival, Miss Maxine!." Kris said

"Me? W-why? How?!" I stammered.

One of the boys, Harley I think, scampered off. He returned not a few seconds later with a worn and tattered magazine. And I made an audible gasp when he held it out with stretched arms into my lap.

It was pornography! Battered, beaten, and bleached from the sun, only a few pages remained. But those that were, were filled with busty blonde women, all eight by eleven square inch.

"Where do you get this? This… this isn't for you boys. You're far too young!" I started up.

"Nuh, uh! We're eighteen!" One of them chirped from the darkness.

"We found it after the crash. In the wreckage." Mickey said plainly.

"That aside boys, I don't see at all how I'm supposed to be so special-"

My words caught in my throat. I had been aimlessly flipping through the pages when the image came before me. It was of a transexual woman, legs spread on a throne of stone. She looked like some sort of jungle queen with an animal print string bikini, full, ample breasts on display, and a large, cut cock jutting out from between her legs.

I gasped.

It was me. Much younger of course, but me all the same.

The fantasy of every boy there for at least a year, I was now sitting there in the flesh before them.

"You see? We knew one day you'd come!" Mickey said.

I was quite speechless. A mistake in college had returned to haunt me. I was angry with my parents and hated their money. I wanted my own. I wanted independence from their fortune. And so I was coerced by a man who convinced me I was his friend. A few dates led to sex, and sex led to photographs. A few weeks later he offered me a chance at more. A chance to stick it to my family. A chance to make 'big bucks' on my own.

And here I thought I had burned every copy…

"You're 'The' Goddess Miss Maxine. It says so. You rule the jungle!" Kris piped up.

Sure enough, superimposed over my glossy mistake, big bold letters spelled out: Maxine, Queen of the Jungle.

"Boys… I-"

Each of them looked up at me. It was like wading through a sea of claw-machine toys. Their eyes sparkled and shimmered, their smiles white and beaming. I was another being to them. Something transcended from a mere human woman.

I held my tongue and sat in silence for a moment, hands on my lap, covering the lewd images. Then slowly, I tucked the magazine away under the bedding behind me, smiled at them, and nodded.

"I'm sorry it took me so long to find you." Instantly, each of their faces lit up. "But now I promise I'll find a way to get you home."

With a shock to my ears the boys erupted in cheers! They clapped and sang, kissed and hugged. It was all a bit off yet thrilling. Surely they lacked some maturity being locked away on this island prison, because in some ways they acted with curious innocence. But as I would soon find, there were other parts quite the opposite.

The boys were quite charming, some a bit more boyish or rambunctious than others. The longer haired teens seemed a bit more effeminate. They wore shirts, or at least scraps of shirts, and their loincloths appeared more akin to a skirt than shorts. They seemed to be the ones that cooked or served food, while the short haired boys were all topless, more lean, and carried themselves like men.

Over dinner I felt I had to tell them that I heard nothing about any search, but that those kinds of things often didn't get broadcast to the outside world, but that I was sure their parents were searching for them even as we spoke.

I had no idea if that was true, but I didn't want to say anything that might dash their hopes.

We talked some more, but as the sky darkened the boys began yawning. As the fire swindled I was greeted by Mickey and Kris again. They simply walked up, holding hands, and stood in front of me.

"Come on, Miss Maxine, we've prepared a bed for you," Kris said, taking my hand. He smiled at Mickey as I stood. I assume I was just being led back to my tent, perhaps by the defacto 'leaders' of their little tribe. But after we entered, and I refocused on the single cot-like bed, reality began to sink in.

Kris drew the sash next, engulfing us in the amber glow of candle light. I stood there, frozen in the center of the room, watching in disbelief as the two boys disrobed, unveiling a pair of smooth, curvy bodies. Mickey was lean and athletic, with just a hint of muscle, while Kris was trim, with child bearing hips, pert nipples and a gorgeous, heart shaped ass.

This wouldn't be awkward or anything.

"You're not going to sleep with your clothes on, are you?" Mickey asked.

I hesitated, clinging to what was left of my shirt and jeans.

"Of course she isn't. Here, let's help her." Kris said.

Before I could react, the boy's hands were on me. Not groping or fondling, but tugging at my hems and fidgeting with my buttons.

"W-wait, boys!" I blurted, but it didn't matter. A second later and my outer clothes were tossed askew. In nothing but a bra and panties, their little fingers went back to their task.

Slower now, I felt their probing hands. Mickey unclasped my bra and slid my one, surviving strap over a shoulder. Kris knelt as he peeled my panties down, eventually unveiling my thick, semi-hard cock to the tent.

"Ooohhh," Kris said, "she's so big!"

I bit my lip, unsure, nervous, and panicking briefly.

"Even bigger than in the magazine! It looks yummy!" Mickey said.

When my clothes were gone, I stood there naked, trying (unsuccessfully) to cover my nudity. My breasts were one thing, using my arm as a hand-bra to cover my hardening nipples, but the eight inch python dangling between my legs was another battle entirely.

Once I was fully nude the pair guided me down the soft, furry bed. It was unexpectedly comfortable, if not a little cozy for a grown woman who'd been sleeping in a raft for the past week. But my body was wrapped in smooth, fuzzy hides that were surprisingly cool in the humid air. Once wrapped in the blankets, Mickey and Kris coiled around me on either side. Their smooth bodies sent shivers along my spine as they adjusted and coiled around me. Their hands explored briefly, each finding one of my large, plump breasts before squeezing. Once more they did not grope, but after a few short kneedings let their hands simply rest on my bosom.

It had been so long since I'd been touched like that, and I was quickly lulled to sleep with the comfort of it all.

I awoke in the dark, confused, unsure of where I was. The dim flickering light of the candle's fire brought me some awareness - I was on a deserted island with a group of boys who have mistaken me for some sort of god. Then the stimulus that awakened me reasserted itself - a pair of soft lips around the head of my cock, gently suckling with practiced moves. A tiny tongue between them twirled and slavored, soaking my glans so that the lips could sink deeper.

I bent my head to see who it was, when Mickey's cute, cherubesque face hungrily bobbing on my thick, fat cock, barely able to fit the meaty tip into his little mouth.

"Mi-Mickey!?" I gasped, biting my lip, wanting to stop him but unwilling to thwart him at the same time. "What are you doing?!"

He sucked and licked a few more times before gripping my rod in his tiny hands and smiling up at me. "Pleasing you, my Queen. Am I doing a good job?"

The boy's eyes sparkled, reflecting the flickering candlelight back at me. I huffed again, mind a blur, knowing he shouldn't be doing this, knowing it was wrong. But my lips and words defied my sanity, "Y-yes... don't stop."

Mickey smiled wide, quickly taking my glistening tip back between his lips. He kissed it once, twice, then popped it back into his mouth, putting his tongue to work once more.

I ran my fingers through his hair, caressing his head as he worked. Suddenly I felt another, second head dip under my other palm, then a second set of lips on my cock. It was Kris, joining his (lover) to bathe my womanhood. One of them was amazing, both were divine - two tiny tongues licked and slathered me root to stem. I held each of their dainty heads, guiding them in all the places I willed their tongues go.

It had been so long... years perhaps, since my last orgasm. And now not one, but two succulent mouths ground together, expertly sucking my cock, drawing in my long, hard shaft, immensely full of cum, slipping warm, wet lips up and down in a strange, exotic rhythm, their tongues teasing my slit and the underside. From the rumbling base of my steely shaft, up the long, silky pleasure rod, to the plump dick head Kris began deepthroating me, velvet and steel both. His fingertips grazing the underside of my full, swollen balls, tickling and teasing me there.

I groaned with pleasure and the boys seemed to redouble his efforts, firming the pressure of their lips on my increasingly sensitive and responsive cock. I could feel pre cum flowing from my slit to mingle with the saliva in his mouth, and I knew the time was close.

Clearly they were no stranger to oral sex.

At that we became a pile of eager, lust-filled flesh, my womanhood anxious for completion, for the fulsome pleasure of jetting my semen into their openings and across each other's bodies. I returned my hand to Mickey's head, pushing my pulsing ten inches of hard, hot meat down his throat.

They alternated in their fellatio, guided by my commanding grip. When one throat was enough, I would lift one tiny boy's head off of my spear and drive another down after, forcing the former onto one of my smooth, hefty balls.

Kris sucked harder, stroking my long, angry shaft as his mouth worked my cock head, until the ecstasy was too much for me and I grunted, shoving my entire length down the boy's throat in a heaving, groaning climax.

"Oh, fuck! I'm… I'm cumming!" I gasped, letting loose a feral growl.

If he heard me, and I don't see how he couldn't have as the whole camp must have been alerted, Kris did not waver. No doubt he wanted to catch as much of my hot girlcum in his mouth as possible. The thought of a young boy wanting my cream brought me over the edge and I shot what felt like gallons of hot jizz into his mouth and down his throat. I forced his head down while I pumped, bucking my hips to fuck his delicious mouth.

All at once, our bodies shifted into a slower gear, rocking and caressing each other simply by touch and nearness. I felt more relaxed and content than I had in years. It was a revelation, and I felt true bliss for perhaps the first time in my life.

Then in my moment of euphoria, I shivered as Kris slowly slid his mouth's grip off my cock.

I felt the boys move. Mickey laid next to me and Kris brought himself up until his face was next to ours, intimately kissing each of us, thrusting his creamy, cum covered tongue into my mouth.

Suddenly and swiftly, Mickey rose to his knees, thrusting his pelvis into the air in front of us. His rock hard, four inch penis throbbed mere inches from my face. I stared at it a moment. Surely he didn't want me to-

Kris interrupted my thoughts, quickly scampering on top of me to take Mickey's hardon to his plump, girlish lips.

I laid there as Mickey slipped his dick between Kris' wet lips and began fucking his lover's mouth. Enjoying the view of a boy's hard, saliva-covered cock slipping in and out of another boy's sucking mouth, his wet and slick ball sack bouncing on his lover's chin, I nearly came again. Kris' lips and tongue worked to bring the ultimate pleasure, and both boys moaned with mutual euphoria, their gasps and groans increasingly louder as passion took control of them.

My hand found my own cock as I watched. To my surprise I was hard again, so I slowly stroked my meaty girth as I watched the loving blowjob so close to my face.

Soon though, Mickey could not control his pleasure long and moaned, "Krissy baby. I'm cumming! I'm cumming Krissy!"

On cue, 'Krissy' sucked harder on his lover's penis. He moaned as Mickey cried out in a high pitched squeal.

Pulses of cum shot from Mickey into Krissy's grateful mouth, and the girly boy swallowed it all. When their convulsing subsided, the two boys slithered down next to me. Kris laid on top of me, enveloped by my breasts, then kissed us both.

Mickey's creamy kiss was an especially hot nightcap before I fell into deep, coital slumber…

The End (of Part One)

ABOUT THE AUTHOR

Jordan Bailey

Jordan Bailey is a transwoman originally from England who now lives quietly in the United States. Her hobbies include writing, movies and playing with her dogs. Lover of anime, manga and animals, she primarily writes about Futanari, or 'Dickgirl' women and crossdressing. She also enjoys weaving tales about effeminate young men, a.k.a. 'femboys', transwomen and other transgender themes!

To get updates, send feedback, or anything else, follow her on Twitter @tehjordanbailey

www.ingramcontent.com/pod-product-compliance
Lightning Source LLC
Chambersburg PA
CBHW082048220626
47052CB00007B/1254